THE LAST TO KNOW

Book Two of the Hallowed Halls Series

By

Mary Alford

Whoever fights monsters should see to it that in the process he does not become a monster. And if you gaze long enough into an abyss, the abyss will gaze back into you. ~Friedrich Nietzsche

COPYRIGHT

DEDICATION

To Jane Squires, who is the inspiration for the character Jane Keller. Thank you, Jane, for all your support!

SCRIPTURE

John 1: 5
And the light shineth in darkness; and the darkness comprehended it not.

DEAR READER

I hope that you will enjoy Cooper and Hannah's story as their search for the Embalmer Serial Killer leads them toward freedom from their past secrets. If you enjoy The Last to Know, I hope that you will check out the first book in the Hallowed Halls series, Don't Close Your Eyes. And be sure to watch for the next book in this series, See No Evil!

PROLOGUE

He'd promised. Sworn the last time would be the last time. He'd lied. The throbbing pain coursing down the right side of her body and the dark bruises under her eye served as vivid proof of the deadly extent of those lies. They stared her in the face just as clearly as the choices she must make.

To stay would all but guarantee death. To leave would mean he'd follow through on his promise to track her down no matter where she went. Even to the ends of the earth. Even though the third choice was unimaginable, it was the only real choice left after all . . .

◆◆◆

Hannah London fought and clawed her way back to consciousness. A scream tore from the space where the nightmare held her hostage, reverberating off the walls in her head. If she stayed there much longer, something she'd feared for years would be revealed. Once the monster came out into the world, the horror he had kept secret couldn't be returned. The genie would be out of the bottle.

Hannah's head shot up off the pillow, her pulse racing a mile a minute.

"A dream. Only a dream." She wasn't back in Jamestown in that tiny apartment shared with her father, mother, and older brother.

Soon, images took shape through the darkness. Her dresser. Armoire. She was home in Alexandria, Virginia, a short distance from where she worked as part of the BAU, the FBI's Behavioral Analysis Unit.

Hannah clicked on the lamp next to the bed. Darkness fled. Familiar objects she'd carefully chosen for the room made it easier to believe the nightmare was just that.

She'd had the same dream since she'd almost died at age twelve. Yet, deep down inside where the truth existed, something wouldn't let her accept the dream as reality.

The clock on her phone proclaimed it was just past two in the morning. Exact time of her transplant. Even after nineteen years Hannah remembered every detail of what led up to getting her new heart.

She'd fought death her entire life. Even at a young age she'd known at some point a transplant would be the only way she'd survive. Still, when it happened, Hannah had felt life leaving her body. At that moment one thing had become clear.

She wanted to live.

Thankfully, a heart had become available. Someone had died so that she could live.

She swung her legs over the side of the bed and slipped into her warmest robe. The January chill had set in around the city, holding it hostage with an icy grip. Spring thaw seemed months away.

And Hannah was scared.

She drifted through the house like a ghost flitting from room to room. At times, she felt like a ghost. Never really engaging with others because of her uncertain future. Surrounded by happy people living happy lives, when hers was lightyears away from theirs.

Every beat of her borrowed heart reminded her time was precious.

Its steady cadence ticked off the truth. She was living on borrowed time.

◆◆◆

Sweat beaded his brow. His hand shook on the shotgun he held. Her screams echoed up the stairs of the basement, piercing his heart.

He reached for the doorknob. His thirteen-year-old mind struggling to understand what was happening. Tears streaming down his face.

"Mom." Please let her be okay.

He opened the door. His eyes adjusted to the dimness. The truth unfolding wasn't possible. He couldn't wrap his head around what was right before him.

There was blood. So much blood.

"Mom!" he screamed and descended the steps.

Her frantic eyes met his. His mother sat on the floor, throat slit. Her body bloody and covered in cuts, but still she tried to protect him.

"Mom." He hiccupped her name. It took more strength than he knew he possessed to not run back up those steps.

He raised the shotgun.

"Put the weapon down. I can explain." The person responsible for harming his mother wasn't a stranger.

Cooper raised the shotgun, resting it against his shoulder like he'd been taught. His finger trembled as he placed it on the trigger.

"Don't do it." The knife in the attacker's hand became larger than life as he held it higher.

Cooper didn't budge.

The man suddenly charged.

Cooper pulled the trigger. A single shot blasted through the air, striking its target. A loud thud followed. Gunsmoke assailed his senses. Tears blurred his vision.

His mom's head lolled forward. Even before he reached her side, he knew the truth. She was dead.

An animalistic wail filled the room. Cooper Delaney sat up in bed, his breathing coming hard and fast—like always.

His head screamed he wasn't that thirteen-year-old boy anymore. He was a grown man who'd done his best to put the horror behind him. Mostly, he'd accomplished this goal. Cooper was a member of the FBI's Behavioral Analysis Unit. He loved his job. He hadn't let the past define him.

Yet at night, when he was all alone, the truth refused to remain buried.

The person responsible for harming his mother wasn't a stranger. It was someone she trusted. Someone Cooper thought he knew better than anyone. Someone he didn't know at all. His father.

CHAPTER ONE

Staley Road, Grand Island, New York—0300 hours

Headlights flashed along the winding, tree-lined drive. She was home. Right on time. The excitement of the kill diminished slightly with the decision he'd need to make. Follow his cravings or Mentor's wishes.

Mentor had been bragging about his "pretty ballerina" for years. Insisting she'd make the perfect addition to their family.

Only *he* knew the truth. Giselle Witherspoon was far from perfect and not worthy of being family.

He slipped behind one of the black cherry trees near the sprawling mansion she'd lived in alone since she and her husband separated.

As the car neared, its driver punched the garage door opener.

He peeked out in time to see her sleek, dark blue Mercedes slide into the garage. The door closed.

He waited.

Lights turned on inside the home. He stood outside the living room peering through the sheer curtains that allowed a view of the room and the kitchen beyond.

She staggered and caught herself, hiccupping out a giggle. Drunk again. His mouth thinned. Mentor's promising beauty had an ugly flaw that couldn't be overlooked.

She'd once been one of the most sought-after ballerinas of her time. She'd studied at Julliard and then the Royal Ballet in London. Giselle Witherspoon had danced before dignitaries and royalty. Mentor had seen her in person many times and had spoken about being captivated by her graceful moves.

For a while, her life seemed perfect. Married to a high-powered Wall Street stockbroker, her career at its peak. She was one of the top ballerinas in the US. Then, three months ago, she'd fallen from the stage while rehearsing with the New York City Ballet and injured her knee.

Mentor's Giselle had become a disappointment. She wasn't forged in steel like Mentor believed. She'd spiraled quickly under the use of prescribed painkillers then graduated to alcohol.

Despite Mentor's insistence Giselle was worthy of immortality, he knew differently. Tonight, he'd come for the kill, not the kidnap.

She poured a glass of wine and stumbled to the living room, fumbling for the TV remote. Soon, sound filled the room. Giselle stretched out on the sofa, her toned legs peeking out from her skirt.

Should he wait until she'd passed out to put her out of her misery? No, he decided. As much as his mentor adored Giselle, her weakness only disgusted him, and he wanted her to know how she'd disappointed him.

Mentor would be angry his orders hadn't been followed. He'd deal with that after he'd finished his task here.

Thinking about her pain filled him with excitement and lowered his usually methodic train of thought. He stepped wrong, dislodging one of the white sandstones decorating the flowerbed near the window and it thudded to the ground.

Giselle sat up suddenly and listened, her eyes focused on the window where he stood. Did she see him? Part of him wanted her to. Wanted her to see the nightmare coming her way.

She rose gracefully and crossed to the window. The urge to remain still—to reveal himself to her—was strong, yet he couldn't risk her calling for help.

Instead, he knelt and pressed his gloved hand just below the windowpane imagining her doing the same.

After all of Mentor's praise, he'd gone to see her dance in the city. At the time, he'd imagined a different outcome. One reserved for those deserving. The perfect ones. Giselle was no longer perfect.

Glass shattered. He raised himself up to peer inside. She'd dropped the wine glass on the kitchen floor and tried to pick up the pieces. Her delicate hand dripped blood. The drinking had gotten worse since her husband moved out. Each night she defiled her body with it.

He slipped through the small garage door. She'd forgotten to lock it.

Inside the house, anticipation hummed through his veins. He touched his special tool. It cried out to be used.

"Daniel, is that you?" She slurred her words, too drunk to realize he wasn't her husband.

As he neared, recognition flashed in those exquisite green eyes. "You."

He'd watched her, learned the pattern of where she went. The liquor store where she bought her booze. A restaurant where she occasionally met with friends. The local grocery store.

"Hello, my beautiful ballerina." His voice dripped with sadness. It wasn't supposed to be like this. He'd believed Mentor in the beginning. She would be perfect. She'd let them both down.

Giselle placed her blood-covered hand on her forehead as if trying to remember how she knew him. Never mind that a killer stood in her home.

"It doesn't matter. Dance for me. One last time." He could almost feel Mentor's jealousy. He would be the one to witness her final dance.

She sobered a little and backed away, her head wagging. "I-I can't. I'm injured." Her huge green eyes held his. "How do you know I'm . . . I was a dancer?"

Next, she would scream—they all did when they realized what would come. Though there were no close neighbors, he couldn't take the chance of someone overhearing.

She grabbed the broken glass from the floor and pointed it at him like a weapon. Her moment of bravado surprised him. Most cried and begged for their lives. Few fought. Usually, he could predict who would do what. He hadn't expected his ballerina to fight back.

"I'm calling the police." She looked around for her phone.

"They won't get here in time." He stepped closer.

The truth dawned in her eyes. She understood he'd come to kill her.

She backed away. Her cell phone lay on the kitchen counter. If she turned, she'd reach it.

"Time to be famous again. You want that, don't you?"

Fear etched itself on her face, yet so did pride. "I am famous."

She still clung to her past glory. He couldn't let her. "You aren't. Soon no one will remember you. You've been replaced. I can make you famous again. I will make it happen."

She lunged for the phone. Before he snatched it from her hand, she hit a number. He grabbed for the phone with his gloved hand while listening to the ring on the other end.

She cried out and slashed the jagged glass against his face. He growled at the pain, his fury growing.

"Giselle, is that you?" A man's voice sounded frantic. He'd heard the struggle taking place. "Giselle."

He hit end on the call and tossed the phone away, his wrath overshadowing his brief admiration at her will to live.

He lashed out, backhanding her. She flew across the room and slammed into the kitchen wall. In two strides he reached her. He stared down at her while wiping blood from his face.

After only a moment she regained consciousness.

"You could have been eternally famous. One of the immortals. Now, you're just dead." He snatched her up to within inches of his face, rage radiating from him.

She shrank away from him, her eyes fixed on his face as if unable to look away.

A slow smile curled his lips. He wanted her to see what she'd unleashed in him before he took it out on her body as only he could do.

◆◆◆

Behavior Analysis Unit Headquarters—Quantico, Virginia—0600 hours

The message read urgent, which translated to all-hands-on-deck. First day back and Hannah London would hit the ground running. Someone had died. But this wouldn't be a normal death. Their team only investigated the worst kind—those perpetrated by serial murderers.

Hannah stared up at the building with a bad case of the nervous jitters. "Get a grip, London. This isn't your first day on the job." Just the first day back since . . .

Grief rolled over her in waves. Ellie, oh, Ellie. Her rock was gone.

"Stop it." Her breath fogged the windshield of her twenty-year-old Volkswagen Beetle.

She rubbed moist hands down the legs of her pantsuit. *This is silly. Everything's the same.* And yet it wasn't. It would never be the same again. Reality had slapped her in the face, shrinking her future to a few precious years.

As far as everyone here knew, she'd been out sick with the flu bug that had hit the city particularly hard. Partly the truth—she had gotten sick.

But mostly it was contemplating the future that kept her away. She'd needed time for that.

What are you waiting for? Just do it.

Yet one thing held her back. One face appeared before her eyes, breaking her heart. Cooper. She hadn't meant to hurt him. She loved him. Had gotten greedy. Hannah let herself believe she could be normal. Ellie's death destroyed that myth.

Tears stung. Hannah dug her hands into her palms in a coping mechanism she'd learned early on. "No." She wiped the back of her hand over them. She wouldn't cry. She'd go inside. Do the job she loved and had fought to keep, and she'd find a way to tell Cooper they were over. Over. They'd barely begun. It wasn't fair. Cooper made her feel alive. He gave her hope.

"Stop feeling sorry for yourself. Get out. Get it over with. You can do this." She shoved the car door open and climbed out, closing it a little harder than necessary.

"Sorry, Millie." She had tender feelings for the Beetle she'd gotten in college.

Though she'd technically recovered from the flu a week earlier, the devastating news that came on its heels had made it impossible to face her friends at BAU and not fall apart.

Each had called to check on her, including Cooper.

Her lengthy recovery time had created suspicion from her commander, Jack Montgomery. Jack knew she ate, breathed, and slept BAU. Being gone for more than a few days wasn't like her.

Zeke, her brother, had given her the heads-up that Jack and his wife, Megan, were coming over.

The minute Jack got a good look at Hannah, he knew this was more than the flu. In a moment of weakness, she'd blurted everything out—assured him her doctor cleared her for duty—and begged him not to fire her.

After speaking with Doctor Robinson, Jack was convinced enough to keep Hannah on as primary profiler for their unit on the condition she kept him updated on how she felt, and if he ever believed it was too much for her to handle, he'd bench her. No questions asked or, as he'd said, no arguments.

Hannah willingly agreed because the job and her brother—and her mother back in Pennsylvania—were all she had.

A sigh tore from deep down where her broken spirit rested. She started toward the building, dreading the first day back questions.

Might as well get it over with.

Out of the corner of her eye, someone approached. Hannah braced for the confrontation she knew was coming with Cooper.

Instead, Zeke fell into step beside her. Five years older, at times Zeke had been more of a parent than either of theirs. He'd practically raised her when their father left and their mother checked out.

"Glad you're back." Zeke gave her a hug, which was about as out of character as it got. Zeke wasn't much on showing emotion. It was how he dealt with their family issues. "You got the message?"

Zeke swept back a curly lock of blond hair from his forehead and pushed his glasses up on his nose. Dressed in khakis and a button-down shirt, the collar of his heavy wool coat turned up against the cold, Zeke reminded her more of a college professor than a BAU agent.

"I did. And I'm glad to be back." The truth mostly.

Looking at Zeke was almost like peering into a mirror. Hannah was the female version of her brother, right down to the silver-blonde hair and green eyes flecked with gold. Nearly as tall, she'd lost ten pounds recently, and it showed. Her clothes hung from her frame. Hannah could practically see her ribs. The skinny girl she'd seen in the mirror that morning reminded her of the worst moment in her life. She'd almost died. Actually had for a few minutes.

With crimson-gloved hands Hannah gathered her coat closer to fight off the biting cold that seemed to bore right through her clothing. She yanked the red knit cap lower.

"Ready for the questions?" Zeke attempted humor when nervous.

Which meant there was something he wasn't telling her.

She turned his way and tried to figure out what he was hiding. Zeke was a hard read most times. He kept his feelings close to the vest.

"No, but I'm used to them."

Ellie's sweet face popped into her head, and she stuffed down the sob. She and Ellie had met at a support group for transplant patients.

They'd both gone through a heart transplant. Now Ellie was dead, and learning of her friend's death scared the daylights out of Hannah.

"Ellie's fate isn't yours," Zeke reminded her.

But it might be.

Zeke held the door open for her. Other than her brother, Jack and Megan were the only ones who knew her secret. Megan was like a sister. Hannah had trained as a profiler under Megan's skilled tutelage. Although Megan had left the unit after her marriage hit a bad patch following the Angel case, Hannah still kept in touch. She and Megan shared everything. Which was why Hannah's secret had hurt her friend. Hannah was still working on rebuilding Megan's trust.

There was someone else who deserved to hear the truth from her soon even if she wasn't ready to share it. She'd been dodging Cooper's calls because she didn't know what to say to him. She and Cooper had been dancing around the edges of romance for a while now. They'd flirted forever. Started dating. Shared a kiss that made Hannah believe maybe her life would be okay as long as she had Cooper in it. Spending time with him made her happy. She believed he felt the same way.

She cleared her throat. "Any idea what this is about?"

"None," Zeke assured her as they entered the building and headed for BAU offices. The place was empty, but not really. Team members had gathered in the conference room. Hannah did her best to steady herself before she stepped inside and joined the game again.

CHAPTER TWO

His heart hit the floor the minute she came into the room. He'd known today would be Hannah's first day back—Zeke had warned him. Cooper told himself he was ready to face her, no matter how awkward it might be or what the outcome. That all crumbled around him now.

When they'd first started dating, Cooper told himself he wasn't the type to let a woman get under his skin . . . except it was all a lie. She had gotten to him.

He'd done his best to be patient when Zeke told him Hannah had the flu, but patience wasn't his strong suit. His last memory of Hannah was kissing her. The taste of her lips. The way her eyes had darkened. Her soft cheeks. Wind whipping her blonde hair into her eyes. It had all been branded in his memory, haunting him at the most inconvenient times. When his calls went unanswered, he'd left a couple of messages that weren't returned either.

As much as he wanted to bring his partner, Zeke, into his misery, he hadn't. Instead, he'd contemplated everything he'd said to her. Cooper wasn't always the most tactful when he wanted something, and he wanted Hannah. Had he overstepped her comfort zone by kissing her?

Her gaze tangled briefly with his. He raised his brows as if to ask, "What's going on?"

Hannah ignored the unspoken question and Cooper's frustration.

He dragged his attention from her to Jack and the reason they were meeting here in the first place, while the familiar dream from that morning still tugged at his mind.

Cooper had left Rochester and that ugliness behind. Changed his last name. Yet the horror of that day still followed him everywhere he went. He guessed that much evil would have to.

Jack stepped up to the front of the room. "First off, welcome back, Hannah." Jack's chin jutted her way.

Everyone around the table clapped. Bright red color crept up Hannah's neck.

"Glad you're feeling better." Sierra Parker, the newest member of the unit, gave Hannah a hug. Sierra had once been the unit's secretary but had proven herself deserving of the position of agent two years earlier when one of their own, Dan Orlando, turned out to be the Angel killer. Dan's betrayal had rocked the tightknit BAU. That one of their team could be capable of such gruesome violence seemed unthinkable.

Cooper had worked side-by-side with Dan for several years, never suspecting the darkness that lurked beneath Dan's polished exterior.

"I second that." Jane Keller, the new office manager, smiled at

Hannah and gave Cooper a wink, which he ignored. Jane knew he and Hannah were dating and had plagued him with questions about when his "sweetie" would return so he would stop looking like a lost puppy.

In her mid-twenties, Jane's long blonde hair held a pink streak framing her face. During one of the talks, she'd told Cooper she wore the pink in memory of her mother, who'd died from breast cancer.

Jane was smart, computer savvy, and outspoken. He liked that. Cooper never had to question where he stood with Jane.

"Thanks, everyone. I'm glad to be back," Hannah murmured without looking his way again.

A private person, she didn't like the focus on herself. A rare thing, Cooper found, when it came to women. Maybe one of the things that attracted him to her in the first place.

"The reason I asked you all to come in so early is because I had a call from the Grand Island, New York, police earlier requesting our assistance." Jack displayed a photo of a woman on the screen behind him. Everything appeared red around her almost as if someone had splashed red paint, drenching the walls of the kitchen. Only it wasn't paint.

At times, Cooper thought himself immune after so many years of witnessing the awful things this unit saw daily, yet the brutality the victim slouched against the wall had suffered sent waves of disgust through his frame.

"Her name is Giselle Witherspoon. Her husband got a call from his wife that was interrupted. He said it sounded like a struggle on Giselle's end. He and his wife were separated. He lives in New York City, his wife in Grand Island. He became worried when he tried to reach her again and couldn't. He drove out and found her like this."

The woman's head lolled oddly to one side. Her throat had been cut deep, almost to the point of decapitation, speaking of extreme rage.

Cooper sat up straighter, gripping the armrest of his chair as his stomach plummeted.

No. It wasn't possible.

"Why'd the locals call us in? Has there been more than one murder?" Sierra asked the question before Cooper could.

"No. They reached out because of this." Jack brought up another photo of Giselle. Above her head, the killer had written a single word in blood.

Unworthy.

The word jumped from the screen and bored down deep into Cooper's head. It kicked the door open and snatched him back into the past. He was that thirteen-year-old boy again. Unworthy. He could still see it written in his mother's blood every time he closed his eyes. Every time he dreamed.

Don't go there.

"Cooper."

He barely registered someone speaking his name as he catapulted into the darkness. Running down the basement steps. His legs trembling as he stepped toward the screams of his mother . . .

"Cooper." The assertiveness in Jack's voice jerked him from the basement and back to the present.

White spots blurred Cooper's vision. He blinked rapidly while his heart hammered, his breaths becoming shallow and labored.

Focus on Jack. Let it go. He's gone.

The monster was gone. Dead and buried along with his victims. And Cooper's mother.

"Are you okay?" Jack now stood beside him.

"Yeah, sure." Cooper struggled to make his answer convincing.

All eyes were on him, a reminder of the way those in law enforcement had gawked at him after learning he'd been forced to shoot his own father.

A door opened, diverting attention from Cooper. He could breathe normally again.

"Jack, a minute." Megan stuck her head inside, her gaze sliding briefly to Cooper.

She knows.

No matter how hard he'd tried to bury his past, it wasn't going to stay dead. Soon, everyone would know the truth. He was the son of a serial killer.

CHAPTER THREE

"**H**into the hallway, a little surprised Megan called him out. ey, babe, what's going on?" Jack asked when he stepped "I found something you need to see." She turned her iPad to him and keyed in a code. The photo of Ani, their daughter, taken at Virginia Beach this past summer, was replaced by an article from *The Rochester Times* dated twenty-two years earlier. "It's coverage following the capture and conviction of Oliver Ellison, the serial killer known as the Embalmer."

Jack took the tablet from her and scanned the article. Ellison had been caught in the process of killing his final victim, whom he had deemed unworthy. The victim had been Ellison's own wife. The couple's thirteenyear-old son had found her and tried to save his mother. He'd shot his father in the shoulder, but it was too late to save his mom.

"I know most of this. What am I missing?" He frowned as he waited for Megan to drop the bombshell he knew would come.

"Read this." Hannah jabbed one red-coated fingernail to a particular spot on the screen.

"Young Ellison is considered a hero." He glanced up. "So?"

"I did a little digging into what happened to the son, whose name is Cooper." She captured his gaze. Those beautiful dark eyes held a storm inside them. "He was adopted by a family and his last name changed."

Jack held his breath. "It's Cooper. It's our Cooper?"

She confirmed with a nod. "It is. Cooper was that little boy." She breathed out a sigh. "Jack, he shot his father and prevented him from escaping until the police arrived. He is a hero, but I'm wondering if he'll be up to having all this rehashed because we have a copycat mimicking his father's MO."

"Oh wow." Jack ran a hand through his hair. "He never said a word. I wonder why?"

"Well, babe, I can understand why he wouldn't want to relive all this.

Still, you need to speak with him in private before we go any further."

"You're right. He won't want to sit this one out."

Jack strode back to the door and cracked it. He zeroed in on Cooper, capturing his agent's attention. Jack mouthed, "A word." Cooper didn't seem surprised to be signaled out.

Jack went back to his wife and leaned against the wall.

Megan interlocked his pinkie finger with hers. It's funny how that simple touch always seemed to ground him. He loved her so much. Every day, he thanked God she'd chosen to give him a second chance.

Cooper stood before them long enough to see the truth in their eyes. "You know." He scrubbed both hands over his face. "I'm okay. I can handle this, Jack."

Jack didn't answer.

"I've got it under control." Cooper blew out a breath.

"You sure? Because from where I'm standing, you don't have anything under control." Jack closed the space between them and clamped Cooper's shoulder. "I can't imagine what you went through back then losing your mother in such a horrific way and learning about your father's secret identity. I'd understand if you want to back out of this one. No one would blame you."

"I don't want to back out."

"I saw your reaction when you saw that woman," Jack challenged.

Cooper's hands tightened into fists at his sides before he slowly released them. "It threw me, okay. I haven't seen anything about my father's crimes in years. I wasn't expecting it. But I can handle it. I won't let my personal involvement get in the way of working this new case."

Jack wanted to believe his friend. "I can't have you letting it cloud your judgment, Cooper."

"It won't. Whoever killed this woman isn't my father. That monster's dead. There were plenty of others to take his place, like the monster who condemned that young woman on the screen as unworthy. I can handle it, Jack," Cooper said with sincerity.

"I hope you're right, because it appears we have a copycat matching your father's MO and you have a lot of insight into this killer, which will be helpful in capturing him before he kills again. But I need Cooper the BAU agent not Cooper that kid who lived through that nightmare," he stressed.

"You got me—the agent—I promise."

Jack's troubled feeling lessened slightly.

"From what I've seen so far, there are multiple similarities to your father's murders." Jack sensed there had to be more than the display of disappointment from the killer written in that bloody word.

Cooper's hands shook and he shoved them into his pockets and waited.

"The perp's using the catch phrase of your father when he rejected a victim he'd targeted. That's all Embalmer," Jack told him. "In the twentyplus years since Ellison died in prison, there hasn't been a single similar case reported. Clearly, someone has decided to change all that." Cooper slowly nodded. "There's more. There has to be."

Jack slowly nodded. "When I got the call, the police chief in Grand Island mentioned your father's case and the similarity to Giselle's murder. Megan went to work pulling everything we could find about your father's victims." He smiled at his wife. "Embalmer brutally murdered the women he found unworthy and embalmed the victims he found faultless to keep for himself." Jack waited for a response that Cooper struggled to give.

Cooper swallowed several times before speaking, his voice barely audible. "I loved my father. Until that day, I thought he was perfect. He never raised a hand to my mother or myself. He went to every single one of my baseball games. He took me fishing." A bitter smile curled his lips.

Megan touched Cooper's arm. "I'm so sorry."

"Everything changed that day," Cooper said, his tone growing hard. "It wasn't long before I found out he had more victims. Some were branded unworthy. Others were embalmed and found in my grandparents' basement. He'd bricked off a section of the basement and made it airtight to keep them, hoping to preserve them forever." Cooper shook his head. "If he hadn't gone after my mother, I wonder if he ever would have been caught." In Jack's opinion, Oliver Ellison wasn't the type of person to draw attention. He lived a simple life with his family. Had never gotten as much as a traffic ticket. He'd gone to medical school and had become a medical examiner for the county until he'd shifted careers and started working at a neighborhood funeral home. There he'd perfected his embalming skills.

Megan looped her arm through Cooper's.

"We have a possible second victim," Jack said slowly.

"Another woman is missing. Where? When?" Cooper fired off the questions as if struggling to take it all in.

Megan let him go and pulled up the details on the iPad. "Her name is Tiffany Beckham. She's a newscaster in Rochester."

"That's less than a hundred miles from Grand Island. Did the station report her missing?"

Megan shook her head. "Not initially. Her parents were the first to realize she was gone. They said she was supposed to come for the weekend and didn't. They called the station manager, who went to Tiffany's home. Her car was there. He had a key and went inside. All her things were in place, including her house key and phone. Her purse. He called the police. The parents filed a missing person report shortly before Giselle was murdered."

"Just like my old man's MO," Cooper said with a bitter catch.

"Exactly." Jack had read Ellison's files. The women condemned as unworthy were rejected for reasons known only to Ellison. Whatever those reasons were, it seemed to unleash his fury on them. Their murders were brutal. The women he embalmed had died far more peacefully. There was not a scratch on them. A lethal cocktail of lorazepam and morphine ended their lives. It appeared from the medical examiner's estimated time of death Ellison kept his victims alive for several days.

"If he has Tiffany, she might still be alive," Cooper said.

"It's possible. We need to get there and start working the case. I'm going to have to explain your connection to the original perpetrator." Jack tried to gauge Cooper's reaction.

"I know," Cooper said at last, a sad smile on his face. "All my life I've lived in the shadow of my father's crimes. I did my best to move out of that shadow and fought to make sure something good came from the darkness my father created."

Jack understood how destructive that kind of evil could be. He'd gone through it in his own life with the Angel case. It drove him to the bottle and almost cost him everything. He couldn't imagine the guilt Cooper carried with him.

Cooper had tried for more than twenty years to forget the actions he'd been forced to take to stop a monster. Now, like it or not, he would have to face those demons head-on, and it would take everything inside him not to crumble under its weight.

CHAPTER FOUR

Images of Giselle's gruesome death were still on the screen when Cooper returned to his seat. The face of a woman he didn't know morphed into one he couldn't forget. His mother's. Ivy Ellison's dead eyes stared back at him.

Megan and Jack had followed him back into the room.

"We believe the murder of Giselle Witherspoon shows similarities to an old serial killer case dating back more than twenty years earlier," Megan said, addressing the team. Her fingers tapped across several keys, and his father's first victim appeared on the screen, replacing Giselle.

Cooper steeled himself to face his past. All the ugliness leading up to the final moment when the curtain had been ripped away and the truth was there for everyone to see.

Megan's gentle gaze found Cooper. She was like the sister he never had and one of the most caring people he knew. "The killer, known as the Embalmer, stalked his victims for weeks—possibly longer. They were all women and people he seemingly admired. For reasons known only to him some were deemed unworthy, as in the case of our victim, Giselle."

"That's awful," Sierra said. "That's one sick individual. It's like he's playing God or something. Kind of like Dan tried to do."

Cooper flinched. Dan Orlando had believed himself to be God. He'd created angels, and, like the Embalmer, he decided if they were good or bad angels.

To this day, Cooper didn't understand how he'd never seen the real person his father had been. His father had done everything with him. Was his Boy Scout troop leader. A deacon at their church. Oliver Ellison worked hard. Treated his wife like a queen. Cooper still couldn't reconcile the monster who had killed his mother and the others with the gentle, caring man he'd called Dad.

"Serial killers are often able to compartmentalize their desire to kill," Hannah spoke up. "I've talked to many family members of killers. Several said they had no idea their loved one was capable of such violence."

"What about the victims who weren't labeled unworthy by the Embalmer?" Zeke asked. Cooper glanced over at his partner Zeke mouthed, "You okay?"

Cooper nodded, a lie Zeke wouldn't believe. His partner had witnessed what happened earlier. He'd know this case was somehow connected to Cooper.

Cooper had tried so hard to keep his past hidden from the world. Every time someone asked about his parents, he spoke about his adoptive parents. They'd taken him in, despite being the son of a killer, and had loved him. Through their help, he'd had a somewhat normal life.

"They were found after Embalmer was convicted for the unworthy victims' murders," Cooper said. "Oliver Ellison had been sentenced to five counts of life without the possibility of parole."

"My biological father, Oliver Ellison, was the Embalmer," Cooper blurted out. All eyes were immediately on him, including the woman he'd been on the brink of falling in love with.

He glanced around at his friends. Sympathy seeped into their eyes. All for him. Each had seen the breadth of evil existing in the world. Everyone on the team understood that it sometimes disguised itself as good and, like sin, wormed its way into the lives of the unexpected.

"Did you have any idea?" Zeke asked, no doubt wondering why Cooper hadn't shared about his past before.

"None." And he hadn't. "My father was always there for me. He and my mother seemed close." He shrugged, remembering that little boy he'd been back then. So innocent. So fragile. Cooper wished he could take all the ugliness away from his past.

His gaze slipped to Hannah. She had tears in her eyes. Pity for him. Not the emotion he wanted from her.

Jack left his place in the corner of the room and stepped to the front beside his wife. "We have a missing woman and a killer with a head start. If this guy is copying Embalmer, we won't have long to find her. Megan will send each of you the original case files and what we have on Giselle and Tiffany. We'll go over both cases in depth on the flight to New York. We leave at 0900 hours. Go home and pack for an extended stay. We have a lot of work ahead of us."

As soon as Jack dismissed them, Cooper rose. He needed to get out of there before more questions came.

Cooper headed for the door, passing the table where Hannah remained seated. Her pity hurt more than the way she'd avoided him earlier.

He stepped out into the hallway and started for the exit.

"Cooper, wait up." Zeke.

Cooper wanted to keep right on walking, but he couldn't. Zeke was more than a partner; he was a friend.

He stopped and slowly turned as Zeke approached. "I don't want to talk about it." Because he didn't. Not now.

Zeke opened the exit door. "That's cool with me. Come on. You can ride with me. We'll stop by your place first."

Cooper didn't argue. His old Mustang would be safe in the parking garage, and he needed Zeke's quiet presence to still the demons in his head.

Zeke hit the key fob. The crew cab pickup's lights flashed.

As they left the garage, Cooper's thoughts went back to Hannah. What had caused this change in her? There would be no answers coming from Zeke. Whatever secrets Hannah kept, Zeke would take them to his grave.

CHAPTER FIVE

His beautiful Tiffany. Everything about her had proven worthy despite Mentor's dissatisfaction with her as a choice for their family.

"She's perfect," he told Mentor.

So unlike Giselle. His lips thinned. Distaste filled his mouth whenever he thought about the way she'd let herself fall from such lofty heights to become little more than a drunk. Instead of working to improve her strength and fight to get back on the stage, she'd wallowed in self-pity and wasted her talent.

Tiffany was different. He watched her now through the two-way mirror that reflected the room. She'd awakened. He smiled. He would get to spend precious time with her. Get to know her hopes and dreams before he made her immortal.

He slipped the key into the lock and stepped inside, carefully relocking the door. He dropped the key into his pocket.

She lifted her head and craned it toward him.

"Hello, my pretty. I'm glad you're awake." He crossed the room to her bed. "I'm sorry that I had to restrain you. I didn't want you to injure yourself."

Terror boiled from deep in her eyes. No worries. She would come to love him the way he did her in time.

"Please. I'm so thirsty," she croaked.

Of course. The drug he used to sedate her would make her thirsty.

He had prepared for this. He poured a glass of water, placed a straw inside, and took it over to her. He put the straw against her lips. She sipped before turning her head away.

"Why are you doing this?"

Another anticipated question. He set the glass on a nearby table. "Because you are special. You deserve this."

Her eyes filled with tears. "Please, don't kill me."

He tamped down his disappointment. They all begged for their lives in the end, but they weren't there yet.

"I'm not going to kill you. I just want to get to know you better. You are magnificent on TV." He'd watched her religiously every evening. "I never miss your broadcast. You are so much better than the one you replaced." Denise had been a bleached-out blonde with a fake smile, who thought herself indispensable. He'd taken care of her. He wanted to pave the way for his Tiffany and he had. To this day, no one knew what happened to Denise. She wasn't even worthy of being one of his unworthy ones.

Tiffany stared in horror at his confession. "You've been watching me? *Stalking* me?" she exclaimed as if the word repulsed her.

"No, no, no," he said. She was twisting everything. He stopped and gathered several breaths to steady himself. "I'm a fan. I can make things happen for you. I already have."

Her eyes widened. "Denise. What did you do to her?"

"That doesn't matter. You are far better than she ever was."

She stared at him with those dark eyes that seemed to drill down to his soul. He wondered if she saw what lay inside.

No, she couldn't.

Not yet. He wasn't ready to reveal that side of himself.

"I'm going to take those restraints off." He pointed to one of the chairs. "Come have a seat."

She still wore the nightgown she had on when he'd taken her from her bed. He'd slipped into her home after disabling her security system. He'd been inside her place many times before he took her. It was how he knew what pieces of furniture to include in her special room.

For the longest time, he'd watched her sleep . . . waiting for that moment when she realized he was there.

Before she could scream, he'd used the Ketamine to knock her out.

Everything so far had gone according to plan.

He untied the leather straps. She rubbed her wrists as if they hurt. He knew they didn't. He'd made sure the restraints were padded to protect her delicate skin.

"Come. I have a special meal prepared for us, with your favorite wine."

She looked at him and then to the door.

"You won't make it. You're not strong enough. And even if you could, the door is locked."

The brief moment of hope he'd seen in her faded.

"Now, enough of that foolishness. Time to enjoy our meal."

She clumsily swung her legs over the side of the gurney. Tiffany tried to stand under her own power, but it was not to be.

"Let me." He carried her over to the chair. "Now, rest while I bring the meal."

He straightened and took in her beauty. He loved beautiful, perfect things. He'd collected them all his life. She would prove to be one of his favorites. Tiffany was so unlike the ones he grew up with.

She dropped her gaze to hands that trembled. Naturally, she was frightened of him. In time that would change.

He crossed the room and left, relocking the door. She would be too weak to leave, but he couldn't risk his beauty escaping.

In the kitchen the timer ticked off the final seconds for the chicken cordon bleu he'd prepared for her. He placed the chicken onto two plates, along with the garlic butter rice and roasted green beans. The cabernet sauvignon was chilled to perfection. He retrieved two wine glasses and placed them on the tray.

As he passed the mirror, he stopped to look. Tiffany leaned her head against the wing chair, her eyes closed. Raven hair splayed against the chair. Just as she'd be when she finally became his forever.

♦♦♦

Someone had been inside her home. The front door stood slightly ajar. Hannah was certain she'd locked it before leaving that morning. She inspected the front of the house. No signs of forced entry.

Hannah dropped everything as a chill sped up her back. Her heart rate went ballistic. She grabbed her Glock and slowly pushed the door completely open before entering the house.

"Clear," she whispered to herself once she checked the living room. Next the dining room. In the kitchen, a single piece of paper lay on the table. Hannah couldn't take her eyes off it. Someone had left a note. She eased toward the pale-blue parchment paper.

Disturbing words spilled from the page, threatening to take her legs out from under her.

Beloved, now that I've found you again I will never let you go. You will be with me soon. Now and always.

The lack of signature wasn't the most troubling. The words sounded old-fashioned. Not something a kid would say. The writer referred to her as beloved. That seemed to indicate he believed they had some type of relationship.

I will never let you go.

Her privacy had been invaded. The writer had probably sat at her kitchen table and wrote that note.

She could still smell his scent. A mixture of Old Spice and BO.

A sick prank? No one she knew would do this. Except for Ellie and Hannah's mother, her friends were her teammates at the BAU.

Hannah finished searching the house. Nothing was missing. No sign of any forced entry. The back door was unlocked. She searched her mind to remember if she'd locked it after she'd taken the trash out. When she couldn't come up with an answer, Hannah realized the intruder's access to her home was all on her. She'd made a foolish, rookie mistake.

That was almost as scary as the break-in.

Hannah grabbed her phone to call Zeke then remembered he'd left with Cooper, and she was perfectly capable of handling this herself.

Instead, she called her neighbor, Bert, a seventy-five-year-old retired postal worker. He didn't have a key to the house. Even though she'd left the backdoor unlocked Bert wouldn't have gone in without having her permission first.

"Hey, Hannah. How are you feeling?" Bert had collected her mail while she attended Ellie's funeral on Long Island. He'd brought her chicken soup when he found out she had the flu. She trusted Bert. He wouldn't have left the note.

"Much better, thanks." She didn't know how to broach the subject, so she just dove in. "You haven't noticed anyone unusual hanging around my place or in the neighborhood, have you?"

"No, nothing. You having trouble over there?"

She wasn't sure what she had yet. "Not really. Just a feeling, I guess."

Bert knew she worked for the FBI. He didn't know the extent of the monsters she hunted.

"There were a couple of break-ins a few weeks back," Bert told her. "The police suspected some local teens might be snatching what they could to sell for drugs. I haven't heard anything lately, though."

Nothing was missing from her place. Was it some teenager's idea of a joke? The language used in the note mocked that suggestion.

"I'm sure it's nothing," Hannah told him, not at all convinced. "Maybe just the remnants of being sick. I'm imagining things." She tried to laugh it off, yet the note certainly had her rattled. "I'm going to be out of town for a few days. Do you mind watching out for the place?"

"Not at all. I'll gather your mail. Let me know if you need anything while you're gone, Hannah."

"I will." She thanked him and ended the call, happy to have Bert's eagle eye watching her home.

Hannah double-checked the locks before returning to the bedroom. She tossed the last of the clothes for the trip into her bag and checked the time. Twenty minutes before her Uber driver arrived.

She carried her bag to the kitchen, where the note taunted her.

Beloved, now that I've found you again I will never let you go. You will be with me soon. Now and always.

Handling the note carefully, she examined it for fingerprints with a scanner. There appeared to be some. She'd bag it and have it fingerprinted when she returned. The type of paper was sold anywhere including Amazon.

Why had the writer targeted her? If it was to scare her, he'd accomplished as much.

Using gloves, she placed the note into a plastic bag and put it into her laptop backpack. Since she lived alone, Zeke had urged her to get security cameras around the place. She hadn't seen the need until now.

The murder in Grand Island needed her full attention. When the case ended, she'd tell Zeke about the note. The two could figure out if this was the work of a kid or a kook.

She unlocked her laptop. The first page of the original Embalmer case leapt from the screen, every bit as horrific as she'd expected.

Including his wife, four women had been brutally killed after being deemed unworthy by Embalmer. Another four had been found in Ellison's parents' basement. Their deaths hadn't been anything close to painful like the unworthy victims. A drug concoction had simply put them to sleep and stopped their hearts. Embalmer had them displayed along a long corridor. Each woman had been placed into an eight-by-ten-foot space, much like the display windows in a department store. The women's spaces held objects from their homes. There had been an actress. A teacher. A nurse. A hairdresser. All were professional women like Ellison's mother.

In interviews, he'd mentioned how he admired his mother growing up. She'd helped supplement her husband's farming income by working as her church's secretary.

Hannah played a video of a prison interview between Ellison and a Bureau psychiatrist. The interview took place a couple of years after his imprisonment.

Ellison claimed he'd branded the women unworthy because of their secrets.

"What secrets are you talking about?" Dr. Garret asked.

The video camera captured Ellison's every reaction, every micro expression. His brows arched ever so slightly. The question baffled him. "They wouldn't be secret if I told you." A smug smile crossed Ellison's face.

"So you choose not to share them with me?"

From the bit of conversation Hannah had watched earlier, Ellison loved talking about himself. Why be coy over his selection process unless something about it might reveal more victims?

Hannah leaned her elbows on the table and paused the video. She studied Ellison's features. An older version of his son. Same sandy-brown hair. Chiseled jaw. The eyes were different, though. Cooper's were brilliant blue, changing slightly depending on his emotion. Sometimes darker when he was laughing. Deep azure pools when he worked a case.

Outside, a horn honked, startling Hannah.

She walked to the window to confirm her driver had arrived to take her to Ronald Reagan National Airport. A small black hatchback car sat out front. Time to leave.

Hannah searched the front yard while trying to suppress the feeling of being watched. The note. This case. Her dreams. All had her spooked. Death was all around her. At times, she felt it pressing in. Waiting to snatch her.

"Stop it."

Her phone beeped a message from her Uber driver.

Hannah closed her laptop and stuffed it inside the carrying case. She grabbed her coat and purse, which held the adjusted heart medication from her doctor along with something to help her sleep when she couldn't. Lately, since losing Ellie, that was often.

After double-checking the locks, she stepped out into the cold day. The snow from earlier had stopped. Still, the temperature hadn't risen enough to melt the blanket of white covering everything.

Hannah rolled her bag over to the car. The driver, a man in his forties, wore a knit cap over his dark hair. Sunglasses covered his eyes. He stowed her bag before holding the rear passenger door open for her.

Guilt riddled her the entire drive. She'd worked with Cooper going on three years. They'd been . . . close for almost a year of that, and yet she had no idea he came from New York like her or that they'd grown up within a hundred miles of each other. She certainly hadn't known the nightmare he'd been through.

"We're here, Miss." Her driver stared at her in the rearview.

"Thank you." Hannah rousted herself and got out. The driver retrieved her bag. Hannah thanked him and started across the tarmac toward the waiting plane.

Zeke's truck was parked in the private parking section near the airstrip that BAU used. There was no sign of Megan, Jack, or Sierra yet.

She climbed the steps, dreading the awkwardness between herself and Cooper.

Inside Zeke worked on his laptop. Her brother glanced up as she entered. "You're the first here besides me and Coop." Zeke's gaze drilled into her. Saying without words what he'd been telling her for a week now: she owed Cooper an explanation.

She spotted Cooper seated at the back. Hannah left her bag with Zeke. Cooper had his eyes closed. As she approached, he opened them. His startling blue gaze held hers.

Hannah slipped into the seat beside him. He didn't look her way. She'd hurt him. Cooper had no idea she believed she was doing what was best for him. As much as she owed him an explanation, now was not the time.

She reached for his hand and entwined their fingers. "I'm sorry. I had no idea."

A ragged breath escaped. He leaned his head against the headrest and turned it her way. "I know. It's not easy to talk about. I loved him. Practically worshiped him. I had no idea he was a monster."

She, of all people, understood the need to keep those secrets hidden. She'd done her best to keep hers locked away from the world. Would her past—like Cooper's—find a way to burrow out of its hole?

"What happened?" She had no right to ask except their case might hinge on Cooper's memory of that time.

She'd listened to part of Ellison's police interrogation when he'd first been arrested. At that time, Ellison seemed eager to talk about his trophies. He hadn't asked for an attorney. He'd taken pleasure in claiming his conquests.

Ellison eagerly named the women he'd killed violently.

When Ellison had been asked about the possibility there might be other victims, he'd clammed up.

The detective asked how he felt knowing his son had been the one to bring him down. There'd been a crack in Ellison's polished exterior.

Her mental analysis halted when Cooper began speaking.

"I was thirteen when I found out the truth. I came home from school. Heard my mother screaming from the basement. Dad kept a loaded shotgun in their bedroom for protection even though we lived in an upscale neighborhood of Rochester. Dad sometimes worked long hours at the funeral home. He was an embalmer, and yes, I realize the irony of that," he said in answer to her raised brows.

A prickle of dread chased along Hannah's spine. Death had walked beside Cooper as well. He hadn't known the double life his father led. What had triggered his mother's attack? Usually, serial killers kept their deviant activities separate from their home lives. Many, like Dennis Rader, had been able to live parallel lives for the most part. One person at home. An entirely different person when they killed. Yet sometimes there were little cracks that showed through to family members.

"I thought Mom was being attacked by an intruder . . . until I saw him. My father. H-he'd butchered her." His voice broke. She squeezed his hand tighter, wishing she could take it all away. "The word 'unworthy' was written above her head in blood. I'll never forget it as long as I live. I relive those moments. I have nightmares about them."

He paused to collect himself. "I thought he was trying to save her until I saw his eyes. Cold and dead. Like the rest of the killers we've captured. Then I knew. He did it. He killed her."

"Oh, Cooper." Hannah leaned her head against his. Felt a shuddering breath come up from deep inside him.

"The man who charged at me wasn't the loving father I knew. The only way I can describe it was like he'd transformed into an animal. I was so scared. I looked into my father's eyes, and I knew he planned to kill me too. Before he reached me, I pulled back the trigger and shot him." Cooper had been forced to take down his own father.

"The shot struck his shoulder." He appeared unaware that he'd pointed out the spot on his own shoulder. "A neighbor heard Mom scream and called the police. They were already on their way when I shot him. They arrived shortly after with EMTs and saved him." Cooper's voice turned bitter. "It was too late for my mother. They pronounced her dead on the scene."

"I'm so sorry."

He absently nodded. "I've lived my entire life in the shadow of what happened that day."

The rest of the team entered the plane.

"There's everyone." Hannah straightened. She went to pull her hand free, but Cooper held her back.

Their eyes met once more. The depth of the pain that had nothing to do with his father and everything to do with her hit her square in the face. "Why are you ignoring me? What's going on, Hannah? I thought . . ."

She had too.

You aren't being fair to Cooper. He needs to know the truth. Zeke's accusatory words rattled around in her head.

"We'll talk soon. Now is not the time."

"You're stalling." He didn't let her go. Cooper was a no bull kind of guy. Yet how did she tell him that he might be the best thing to happen to her and she couldn't see him anymore.

"How are you holding up, Cooper?" Sierra stood beside them. She had a big heart and a loud personality. She didn't always respect boundaries. So far, in the time she'd worked as an agent, she'd proven invaluable, but there were moments when she could work on her discretion.

Cooper released Hannah's hand. She rose unsteadily and moved to the front of the plane, where Jack and Megan were talking to Zeke.

"How's he doing?" Megan asked pointedly. There was still a touch of distance in her friend's tone.

"He's hurting." Hannah looked over her shoulder to where Sierra had taken Hannah's seat. She wasn't sure if she was talking about what Cooper had dealt with as a child or what she'd put him through.

"I can't imagine going through what he did at thirteen," Zeke said, and looked at Hannah. He'd been a teenager when Hannah's heart gave out. Their father cut out soon after Hannah ended up in the hospital, leaving Zeke to step up and help their mother. He'd been forced to grow up quickly.

"Please take your seats and buckle up. We're cleared for takeoff."

Once the pilot announced their imminent departure, Hannah slipped into a seat a couple of rows up from Cooper and Sierra. Zeke sat next to her.

"You doing okay? You look like you've seen a ghost."

Hannah flinched. "I'm fine." That came out sounding angry, which Zeke didn't deserve. Her brother had always been there for her. She touched his arm. "I'm fine. It's just been a day."

The same green eyes stared back at her. "Being back, you mean? Or is something else going on?" Zeke's gaze drilled into her like it had growing up whenever she'd do something that put her health in jeopardy.

She wasn't ready to talk about the note. "Just being back. There's nothing. Stop worrying. We have enough to think about with what lies ahead of us." This case, maybe because of its connection to Cooper, had her uneasy.

The plane taxied down the runway. Under the pilot's skillful control, they were soon airborne. Flight time would be less than an hour before they arrived at Mesmer Airport-NY49 in Grand Island.

Once the seatbelt light went away, Jack called the team to the table up front to review the case. "You should all have the records from the Embalmer case." He looked around. "Hopefully, you've had the chance to study the previous case as well as what we have right now." Everyone confirmed they'd received the information.

"There are other similarities besides the word written above the victim." Zeke had a keen eye for picking out details that sometimes went overlooked. "Giselle Witherspoon was posed in the exact position as the previous unworthy victims."

Hannah brought up their current victim's photo. She selected one of the original Embalmer's unworthy victims—respectfully, not Cooper's mother—to understand what her brother meant. "You're right."

Cooper didn't follow along with the photos. He probably knew them all by heart.

Jack blew up the photo on his laptop. "I see it too. Anything else?"

"The knife wounds themselves. They're unusual. What type of knife was used originally?"

"A bread knife," Cooper said, his voice devoid of emotion. "Also known as an autopsy knife. The type used during autopsies to slice off pieces of organs." All eyes went to their friend. "My father had several from his days working as a medical examiner."

"What made him want to go to work at a mortuary of all places?" Sierra wrinkled her nose. She quickly realized her mistake. "Sorry."

Cooper sat up straighter. "No, it's alright. I'm okay, guys. This— seeing another woman die the way my mother did—well, it threw me for a moment is all." He released a breath. "I was about eight when he changed professions. I didn't think anything of it at the time. Now, I see he probably perfected his embalming skills working late at night. My mom didn't approve of the change because he worked nights mostly. I heard them arguing. She clearly thought it strange. He told her it would give him more time to spend with her and me."

"And did it?" Hannah wondered if Ellison had been using the excuse to hunt his victims.

"Some, I guess. As I said, he was always there for any of my school activities. And we did a lot of things together on the weekends."

"I've gone over the interviews with your father from jail and later from prison," Megan told him. "He shows classic signs of psychopathic behavior. Unlike some serial killers, your father tested in the genius range intellectually."

Cooper nodded. "I've heard. I never watched any of those interviews. Never visited him in prison. The family who adopted me shielded me from the spotlight. They changed my last name to theirs—Delaney—and gave me as normal a childhood as possible for someone whose mother was murdered by his serial killer father, the Embalmer."

Hannah covered his hand with hers. He stared down at their hands before turning toward her. The depth of pain in Cooper's eyes had her forgetting everything she'd promised herself about keeping her distance. He was hurting, and she wanted to make it better.

"Ten minutes until we land." The pilot announced over the intercom.

Jack closed his laptop. Everyone prepared to buckle up. "We're treating this as two separate cases for now. Until we know for certain what we're dealing with, we don't know that Tiffany Beckham has been kidnapped or if she's gone missing on her own free will. We'll need to split up. Megan, Sierra, and I will run with the Beckham case in Rochester. Cooper, you and Hannah and Zeke meet with the Grand Island police. I've asked the chief to meet you at the Witherspoon house and get you up to speed."

"Copy that." Zeke slid Hannah a look, warning that she'd better settle things between herself and Cooper before things became too strained. They'd be working closely together. Personal emotions wouldn't have a place in the case.

She'd find a way to speak with Cooper when the time was right.

The pilot landed the plane, and then taxied to a stop at the small airport.

"One more thing," Megan stopped everyone before they left. "Jane has us booked on the second floor of the Island Breeze Hotel. Jane spoke to the manager who told her at this time of year the hotel is pretty much vacant. She offered us the use of their conference room and anything else we might need during our stay."

"Nice," Sierra said with a wink. "I've never been one of the only occupants in a hotel before."

Zeke grabbed his and Hannah's bags. Hannah tried not to show her irritation at the gesture. Zeke had grown up being protective of her. He'd become increasingly worried about her physical and emotional state following Ellie's passing.

"There are two rental vehicles waiting for us on the tarmac. Keep your phones close. This case is fluid," Jack warned. "We may have more victims turn up if the killer is tracking true to the original Embalmer case."

Hannah slung her purse strap over her shoulder and followed her brother out into the cold day. Clouds gathered above, dark and gray as if a storm were coming. A cold breeze cut right through Hannah's coat. She tugged it closer. Apprehension she couldn't explain had her searching around them. She also couldn't shake the feeling someone watched her.

"What is it?" Cooper asked, looking around as well.

She didn't want to bring her troubles to him. "Nothing. Just taking in our surroundings."

Two black SUVs waited side by side. As they approached, taillights flashed. A younger man dressed in khakis and a pullover with the logo of a car rental agency stood next to one of the vehicles.

"You must be the FBI team from DC. I'm Darren. I spoke to Jane Keller. She reserved two Suburbans."

"I love it." Sierra took one set of keys. "Can I drive?"

Jack shook his head. "Not if you were the only person capable of driving. I've ridden with you before." He took the keys from her. "Thank you, Darren."

Darren handed the second set of keys to Cooper. "No problem. Give me a call if you need anything else. My office is right over there." He pointed to the sign of a popular rental business.

"We will." Jack waited until Darren left before addressing his people. "Obviously, we're playing catch-up. I'm grateful to the chief of police here for picking up the connection to the Embalmer case. Everyone, be careful, and if you need a break, let your team know." His gaze skimmed over Hannah, the point clear. She wasn't a hundred percent no matter how much she might say otherwise.

If it came to it, Jack would pull her out of the field. Yet this was her life. She couldn't let that happen.

CHAPTER SIX

He'd never been to Grand Island. Before the nightmare became part of every waking moment of his life, Cooper had grown up in Rochester. Went to school there until shortly after his thirteenth birthday.

But even though he hadn't been here before, that feeling inside his gut was the same as when he'd been taken to the station in Rochester. Asked dozens of questions he couldn't answer.

"Cooper?" Hannah's tone confirmed two things. She'd been trying to get his attention for a while, and she was worried by his lack of response.

"Sorry. Shall we?"

Zeke took his ability to form an answer as the green light and climbed into the back seat behind Cooper. Hannah went around to the passenger side.

"I've pulled up directions to the Witherspoon house," Zeke told them. "Looks like it's a couple of miles away."

Cooper backed up, left the airport, and turned onto Grand Island Boulevard.

"Staley is coming up in less than a quarter mile," Zeke said. "Turn left there."

Cooper followed his instructions while glancing Hannah's way. She'd been unusually quiet since they got into the Suburban. Was it the case or his past or what he'd done wrong to drive her away?

"There's Staley." Zeke seemed oblivious to the tension radiating from the front seat.

Cooper pushed whatever was wrong between himself and Hannah aside and made the turn. He drove until he spotted the Witherspoon's turnoff.

The road wound through a tree-lined driveway where each curve provided glimpses of a manmade lake.

Once the house became visible, Zeke blew out a whistle. "That's some place." Past a manicured yard, the gray shake-sided house sprawled before them.

A police cruiser and an unmarked vehicle waited for them. Two men and a woman got out as they approached.

Cooper parked a little away from the two officers.

Zeke climbed from the SUV right away.

Before Cooper could follow, Hannah grabbed his arm. "Are you sure you're up to this?" She clearly wasn't.

Cooper reached for the door handle. "Of course, I am. This is what we do, right? The job comes before everything else." Yeah, it was a jab at her, and the way she flinched confirmed it had hit home.

Feeling like a heel at the childish comment, he waited for her to follow.

Hannah glared at him over the top of the SUV, confirming he'd hurt her.

Zeke looked between them. "Whatever you two are fighting about, knock it off." He directed most of his anger at his sister, confirming Zeke knew the reason behind his sister's cold behavior toward him. "We have work to do."

Cooper kept his questions to himself. Zeke was right. They had to figure out what kind of creep would want to copy his father's work.

"Chief Milam?" Cooper addressed the man wearing a uniform.

"That's right."

Cooper shook the man's hand and introduced himself and the team.

"This is Detective Kate Siegler. She's the lead detective on the case. And Detective Alex Jordan. They'll be assisting you in any way necessary."

"I appreciate it." Cooper told the two detectives. "Can you tell us what you have so far?" He'd hold off looking at the crime scene until the detectives had run through the case for them.

"Not much more than what we gave your commanding officer earlier today. The state police lent us access to their crime scene techs and lab since we don't have one ourselves." Siegler seemed young to be the lead detective and all business. With her light-brown hair secured in a ponytail, her brown eyes assessed his team. Her dark-gray business suit, which wasn't something she appeared comfortable wearing, seemed to indicate she might not have been a detective all that long.

"The medical examiner puts time of death between ten and eleven yesterday evening. That lines up with the timeframe her husband gave us. He received the call around ten."

"CSI come up with anything useful?" Cooper asked the detective.

Siegler shook her head. "We haven't found the murder weapon. No knives were missing. He obviously brought the weapon with him and probably took it. No fingerprints. No DNA so far."

"There was evidence that he may have watched her before he entered the home," Detective Jordan inserted. "Some of the plants were tramped down. Techs made impressions of the shoeprint. They'll let us know what type of shoe made it soon."

"Why don't we take a look inside the house now?" Zeke said.

Siegler looked to Cooper for confirmation, assuming he was in charge.

Cooper suppressed a smile. Zeke was the senior agent.

Siegler hesitated briefly. "Absolutely."

"I'll leave you in the hands of my detectives. If I can be of any further assistance, please let me know." Chief Milam shook their hands before leaving.

"Looks like Mrs. Witherspoon left the garage door unlocked." Siegler continued her oratory. "The killer must have entered through here." She opened the door with a gloved hand.

The kitchen was off the garage. Though it had been hours since the murder occurred, the metallic scent, like rust and iron, from the massive amount of blood overpowered all others.

Cooper stopped dead. Everything except that word faded away.

Siegler's voice became background noise to the drumming of his heart. He was back in the basement watching as his mother breathed her lasts breaths.

"Coop? You okay?"

Cooper forced himself to focus on Zeke's face. Perspiration beaded his upper lip. He clenched his hands while trying to steady his breathing. "Yeah, I'm okay."

Zeke wasn't convinced. Past Zeke's troubled expression, Hannah's sympathetic one made him angry. He didn't want her pity. He wanted . . .

"According to Giselle Witherspoon's husband, she had fallen and hurt herself at rehearsal several months back, basically ending her career as a ballerina." Jordan shrugged. "A shame. I saw her perform once." A broken wine glass littered the floor. Signs of a struggle.

"She fought for her life." Hannah pointed to the state of the living room and kitchen. Items were knocked from the end table. A chair had been turned over.

"Giselle's phone was tossed across the room." Siegler indicated a spot on the floor near the kitchen devoid of blood.

"She called the one person she believed could help her." Cooper remembered thinking his father would save his mother.

"Unfortunately, no one could have saved her."

Cooper frowned at the undertone in Hannah's comment while wishing he understood what had changed between them.

"Nothing taken from the home?" Zeke asked Siegler who shook her head.

"No sign of a robbery. The husband did a walk-through."

"We'll need to speak to him." Cooper walked to the living room window. Below he noticed the crushed plants where the killer had hidden and wondered why someone had chosen to use his father's MO after so long. It wasn't as if Oliver Ellison were a particularly famous serial killer. He'd taken lives within a hundred-mile radius of his home. He'd been caught and shanked in prison. There were many more well-known killers out there to imitate. What had attracted the killer to the Embalmer?

He turned from the window. "We need to speak with any prisoner or anyone else who might have spoken to my father while he was incarcerated."

"Your father?" Siegler was clearly surprised.

Cooper didn't choose to enlighten her.

Hannah came over. "What are you thinking?"

"My father may have had an apprentice. Someone with whom he shared the tricks of his trade."

CHAPTER SEVEN

Cooper waited until they were back in the Suburban before calling Jane. "Hey there, Coop. What can I do for you?"

Jane had adapted using the nickname that Zeke gave him, but it was okay. He told her what he needed. "Anyone who might have had contact with my father. I want the names of people who interviewed him. Any doctors who saw him while he was in prison. Visitors. Other prisoners. Anyone."

"I'll get started on it right away." She hesitated. "How are you holding up? This must be hard."

He appreciated everyone's concern, and they were right. It was difficult. But he just wanted to do his job and find the person responsible for killing Giselle Witherspoon.

"I'm okay. Thanks for asking. Let me know when you have anything." He ended the call. "What's our next move?" Cooper reversed and drove away from the mansion.

"I'd like to speak to the husband next," Hannah said. She read something on her phone. "Looks like Giselle Witherspoon was having trouble with pain medication after her injury. There are a couple articles about her seemingly being under the influence while out at restaurants or clubs."

Cooper glanced her way. "Stands to reason. She suffered a knee injury that was severe enough to end her career."

"True. Siegler just texted Daniel Witherspoon's number. She says he's still in Grand Island. I'll call him and set up a meeting."

Cooper glanced in the rearview mirror and noticed a car some distance behind them. It had been there for a while. Just his imagination?

He slowed, drawing Hannah's attention to him. "Anything wrong?"

No need to worry her unnecessarily in case he was seeing killers everywhere. "No, just thinking."

The car sped up and passed. The windows were tinted enough that Cooper only saw what he believed to be a man behind the wheel.

Soon, the car disappeared down the road and his thoughts returned to the case. How had the killer come in contact with Giselle in the first place? Though he told everyone he hadn't watched any of his father's interviews. Shortly after he joined the BAU, he'd come across an interview with Oliver Ellison from a few months before he'd died. The interview had been with a podcaster who wanted to feature the Embalmer case for her listeners. She'd asked how he found his victims. Cooper would never forget what his father said. He'd looked straight into the camera and said he only chose victims worthy of him.

He'd seen an arrogance about his father that he hadn't noticed before.

"Daniel Witherspoon is staying at a friend's house in town. He said we could stop by now." Hannah squinted at the phone, and Cooper smiled. She'd told him she was supposed to wear glasses but hated them. She'd tried contacts, but they didn't work.

She gave him the address.

"Looks like Jack and the team are at Tiffany Beckham's home. They met her parents there." Zeke stuck his phone into his coat pocket. "I hope they find her."

If Tiffany turned up unharmed, then perhaps they were wrong about the copycat and Giselle's killer had accidently copied the signature of a serial killer. But Cooper's gut told him differently. This killer had some connection to the original Embalmer case.

"It's up here on the right." Hannah pointed to a small, white-framed home vastly different than the Witherspoons'.

Cooper pulled up behind a Mercedes, and they got out.

Hannah knocked on the door.

A man answered. Cooper recognized Daniel Witherspoon from several photos he'd seen of the man with his wife during happier times. "Mr. Witherspoon, I'm Hannah London. I spoke to you a few minutes earlier."

"Yes. Please, come in." Witherspoon led them to a small living room. Cooper glanced around at the tiny space, and Witherspoon must have noticed.

"This place is our maid's home. She became our friend over the years. Serena adored Giselle." His voice broke, and he turned away to gather himself.

There were a handful of photos of Giselle, most taken from her many performances.

"We're sorry for your loss, Mr. Witherspoon. Thank you for agreeing to talk to us."

Witherspoon indicated the sofa, and Hannah sat.

Cooper wandered to the window overlooking the road. Cars passed by. One captured his attention. A white sedan . . . like the one he'd seen following them after they left the Witherspoon estate. Another car passed. White as well. Cooper gave himself a mental shake. He was letting the case get to him.

He turned as Hannah asked the difficult but necessary questions.

"How long have you and Giselle been separated?"

She'd known the answer, but it was important to confirm the husband's story matched what had been documented.

Zeke had requested Witherspoon's phone records to pinpoint he was indeed where he said he was and not capable of murdering his wife.

"Three weeks." Witherspoon clasped his hands together. "My wife had a problem with prescription drugs and alcohol. I thought it would get better in time."

"It didn't?" Hannah kept her attention on his face, analyzing every reaction.

"No, it didn't. When the doctor no longer prescribed painkillers, she resorted to drinking." He seemed genuinely in anguish. "I loved my wife. I still love her. But being a ballerina was her whole life. She'd trained for it since a child, and she was one of the best."

"When was the last time you spoke to your wife previously?"

Witherspoon thought about it. "A few days ago. I kept in touch. I always hoped I could talk her into getting treatment. We could save our marriage." He sat up straighter. "Wait, she told me something. Said she had a feeling someone had been in the house before."

This grabbed Cooper's attention right away.

"Did she say why?" Zeke had been documenting Witherspoon's answers.

"She said there were things moved around. She found the remote to the TV in the kitchen." Witherspoon shook his head. "I just assumed she imagined it. They were only minor things, and with her drinking . . ."

"Where had she been the night she died?" Cooper wondered if Giselle had met up with someone who followed her home.

"I don't know. Serena came earlier in the day. She said Giselle was still sleeping. She did the cleaning and checked on her. Giselle got up and ate something. That was around four. I never spoke to her that day. I had a busy workload. I got back to the apartment around ten. Went straight to bed. Then I got that phone call from her."

Witherspoon leaned forward. "There is something else. Giselle told me she thought she was being followed. She said she noticed the same man at several different places she went during the week."

Hannah glanced to Cooper before asking, "Did she get a good look at this man?"

He shook his head. "Not really. She said he was older. Average looks. It wasn't unusual for her to have admirers. She had fans all over the world. Some crossed the line and tried to get close."

This grabbed Cooper's attention. "In what way?"

"Letters. Trinkets. Things like that."

"Did she keep them?" Hannah asked.

"Yes," he told her. "I gave them to Detective Siegler."

They'd have to get them from Siegler. From here on out until proven otherwise, Giselle Witherspoon was their case.

"Can you think of anything else?" Hannah continued. "Anything she might have said in passing that seemed strange?"

Witherspoon ran a hand across his eyes. "Not that I can remember. I have your number. If I remember anything I'll call immediately."

Hannah thanked him and stood. "I appreciate your cooperation, Mr. Witherspoon."

He followed them to the door. "Please find out who did this to her. Giselle had her issues, but she didn't deserve this. She was just trying to get her life back on track. I always hoped . . ." Tears burned in the depths of his eyes. "We talked about working on our marriage. I loved her. Please, find the person who did this to her and make them pay."

The raw anger, hurt, and pain written on Daniel Witherspoon's face was like looking into Cooper's own soul. He'd been there. Felt everything Witherspoon felt. Wanted to exact revenge on his father. He'd often wondered if the police hadn't arrived when they did, would he have done the unthinkable? Would he have become his father?

CHAPTER EIGHT

The shrilling alarm filled the room, interrupting those final precious moments with her. "No, no, no." He tossed the brush he'd used across the room as the computer screen lit up.

They'd come. The ones he'd expected had come quickly. They were searching Giselle's home. Standing where he'd stood when he'd killed her. Analyzing his work as if he were some strange specimen.

Tiffany gasped, drawing his attention back to his girl. Her pretty mouth was open as death came to claim her.

And they'd ruined it.

He swore to himself. "Goodbye, my lovely." He leaned down and kissed her pale lips. Inches from dead eyes that stared right through him.

Death was the perfect thief. It took one's ability to move, to think, to breathe.

"I'm sorry I missed your last breath." He captured them in special jars to display alongside his pretties.

"I will make you perfect in death." He lovingly stroked her high cheekbones. Flawless translucent skin would require the perfect lighting to display it properly.

As the alarm continued to scream their intrusion, he left her side to stand in front of the screen.

When he recognized the one who had been sent to investigate, a satisfied smile spread across his lips. "Perfect."

After he took the necessary actions to ensure her body was preserved, he retrieved the hairbrush and went back to her. Two hundred strokes. He could almost hear his mentor's voice. Not one hundred ninety-nine or two hundred one. Details were important.

He'd followed the instructions carefully when he'd administered the right concoction of medicine to accomplish her death. He'd enjoyed their time together. Hadn't wanted her to suffer.

When the final stroke was finished, her sleek hair shone. "Now, for the correct outfit. We can't have you going into your immortality with the wrong clothes."

Mentor had helped him select the right outfit from several he'd taken from Tiffany's home.

"The red one. To set off her hair."

Yes, red would be perfect.

As he dressed her, the screen displayed the activity taking place at the Witherspoon home. The betrayer was there. Mentor had planned for him to take over one day . . . until he'd destroyed everything by taking her side.

Once the red dress was in place, he straightened the hem and applied crimson lipstick, a touch of blush, and eyeshadow to her face. Then he stood back and looked, pleased with his accomplishments.

"You did well. It's time to settle her in her final resting place," Mentor said, beaming with pride. "Time to find our next beauty."

"Yes." He smiled down at Tiffany. She was beautiful and perfect in every way. She hadn't disappointed him. She hadn't even tried to fight for her life. She simply accepted her fate and her place of honor among the immortals.

"I have someone in mind," Mentor told him. "She will be perfect."

Will? Mentor never referred to his beauties in such a way. As if they weren't perfect yet.

"What do you mean?"

"Trust me." Mentor's smile reminded him of their past together.

"I will trust you." He couldn't wait to see the one that Mentor selected for him. His attention returned to Tiffany. "Come, my pretty. Come see what I have planned for you."

◆◆◆

The Island Breeze Hotel sign became a beacon in the storm that had struck seemingly out of nowhere, dumping inches of snow and taking visibility down to zero.

Cooper pulled up under the whitewashed portico next to another Suburban. "Jack and the others are here."

Hannah forced the door open against the growing wind.

Zeke and Cooper unloaded their luggage.

Hannah retrieved hers and hurried inside.

"You made it." Jack met them at the door. "Weather's getting worse. Looks like we're in for blizzard conditions. Everyone's in the conference room."

Megan and Sierra were in the middle of discussing the case.

"Did you get any deeper insight into what might have happened to Tiffany?" Hannah shed her jacket and draped it over the chair before she sat.

"Not really. We spoke to her parents, who insisted she would never have simply disappeared on purpose." Megan glanced down at her notes. She documented everything no matter how small it seemed. She'd told Hannah once that was her way of processing a scene.

"There was something weird, though." Sierra wrinkled her nose. "Some of her clothing was missing."

"Really? Were they sure?"

"Yes, positive. Mrs. Beckham said she and Tiffany went shopping a lot. She knows her daughter's wardrobe in detail."

"That's nice they're so close." Hannah thought about her own mother. After her father left, her mother fell apart. If it weren't for Zeke, Hannah wasn't sure how she would have survived being in the hospital for weeks and then all these years on medication, careful about everything she did. Praying her body wouldn't reject her new heart. After a while, her mother had simply disappeared emotionally.

"She gave us a list of three dresses that were Tiffany's favorites," Megan told them.

"Could she have taken them to the cleaners?" Hannah wondered aloud.

"We're checking. Mrs. Beckham said Tiffany sometimes used one of the dry cleaners near her home."

"Why would Tiffany's kidnapper take certain items of her clothing?"

"That's part of his MO. My father did the same."

All eyes shifted to Cooper. He claimed the seat beside Hannah. "His victims were all career women. For those he considered worthy to be part of his private collection, he liked to dress them in clothing that reflected their professions. For instance, he had a nurse wear her scrubs. An actress was dressed in the clothing she wore during one of her last roles."

Giselle hadn't been dressed in her ballet costume because she'd been regarded unworthy.

"Did your father ever have contact with any of these women prior to kidnapping and killing them?" Zeke poured coffee and brought it over to the table, pulling out a chair.

"I'm not sure. Like I said, I never talked to him after that day. The only time I saw him was during the trial when I had to testify about what happened."

Hannah reached over and squeezed his hand. He clasped her fingers. She didn't pull away. Maybe they both needed each other's comfort today. She kept remembering the bizarre note she'd received before leaving home. As much as she wanted to believe it was the work of kids, she didn't.

Once she returned to DC, she'd set up some security cams around the place.

"With the storm we won't be able to go anywhere for a while. This will give us time to go at the case from several angles." Jack glanced around at his people. "I think we all can agree we're dealing with a copycat who has detailed knowledge of the Embalmer's MO. I realize a lot of this was published after Ellison's death, but it appears our killer was a student, at the very least, of Ellison's work."

Jack's attention went to Cooper. "Jane sent over prison records from your father's time there. There's also a list of people who would have had contact with him, including guards and medical staff. Visitors. I thought you
and I could go over the names. Maybe one will jump out at you."

Cooper nodded.

"Zeke, Detective Siegler brought over the letters and trinkets Giselle Witherspoon received from fans through the years. I'd like you and Sierra to start on them."

"Hannah and I can review interview footage from when Ellison was captured and during his prison time." Megan looked Hannah's way. "There might be something in them to help our case."

"Sure." Hannah agreed.

The team broke off in their assigned groups, but Cooper didn't move. He still held her hand. She could almost feel the weight that reliving his father's crimes had piled on him.

"How are you handling all of this?"

He shook his head before facing her. "I thought I'd come to terms with what my father did. I'd moved on. Put it all behind me." "But you haven't," she said gently.

"No, I haven't. I just buried it down deep and pretended it didn't exist."

"If you want to talk, I'm here." Hannah noticed Megan coming their way. "I know we have other things to talk about as well, but why don't we table that discussion for another time? When we get a break, let's talk about your father."

He smiled. "I'd like that. Thank you, Hannah."

Megan hung back as if sensing their conversation might be personal.

"I'll find you. Maybe we can grab something to eat." She squeezed his hand again before pulling hers free.

"There's a small breakroom we can use."

"Alright." Hannah retrieved her laptop and walked with Megan to the room.

"Everything okay between you and Cooper?" Megan asked casually.

Hannah wasn't ready to have this conversation with her friend just yet. It still hurt to know there could be nothing deeper than friendship between herself and Cooper.

"He's just struggling with all this. It's hard having the worst time of his life brought up."

Megan claimed the seat next to Hannah. "I can understand. I carried the awful things my father had done to my mother with me for a long time. Not dealing with it seemed easier. And then Dan came along, and it couldn't stay buried any longer. Not since I learned Dan was my stepbrother after the awful things he did killing so many innocent women. Kidnapping my daughter to lure me out." She stopped and pulled in a breath. "I guess I'm saying I know it's painful for Cooper, but in the long run it will be easier if he gets it out."

Hannah's phone chirped an alert, capturing her attention. Her doorbell camera had gone off. She focused on the front door. Nothing. The wind had picked up blowing the trees near her front porch. Had it set the camera off?

"Something wrong?" Megan asked, catching her apprehension.

"I'm not sure." She zoomed in closer and saw it. A heart-shaped rock appeared near the edge of the porch. How long had it been there? She squinted at the rock and realized something had been written on it in red paint.

You have my heart, beloved.

"Hannah?"

Hannah's hands shook as she slid the phone into her pocket. "Sorry, it's nothing. Just the wind setting off my doorbell camera."

Megan searched her face. "You sure? You know you can tell me anything."

How could she tell her friend that she had a feeling death was coming for her. She'd believed her transplanted heart would give out like Ellie's had, but what if she were wrong? What if the person who had left that heart wanted hers in exchange?

CHAPTER NINE

So far, none of the people who visited his father in prison were familiar. Cooper rubbed his tired eyes. They'd been at it for hours without any luck.

"I'm going to have Jane get us a phone number for Doctor Melendez. Looks like she treated your father multiple times for diabetes. Did you know he had it?"

"No, I didn't. He never talked to me about it, and my mother hadn't said a word."

"Maybe Doctor Melendez will remember something your father might have said." Jack sat back in his seat. "It never ceases to amaze me that serial killers can garner such a following."

Cooper didn't understand it either. There were at least six women who wrote his father in prison. Two men whose letters spoke of admiration.

Most of the women had proven harmless. One of the men had been ruled out. The second didn't answer.

While Jack spoke to Jane about the doctor, Cooper dug deeper into Harold Salcedo, the remaining man to send letters to his father. He tried Salcedo's phone again without any luck. "This is interesting," he said after Jack ended his call. "Salcedo lives about twenty miles outside Grand Island."

"You're kidding. Show me." Jack came over and looked at the location where Salcedo lived. "We need to go there as soon as the weather allows. What does he do for a living?"

Cooper did a further search. "He's a pharmacist. Apparently, he flunked out of medical school."

"He might know how to embalm." Jack held his gaze.

"He could be holding Tiffany Beckham at his house. This can't wait." Cooper rose quickly and grabbed his coat, shoving his arms into it. So far, the full force of the storm hadn't hit. Maybe they had time to reach Salcedo's home first.

"Call Chief Milam. Have him meet us over there. And we need a warrant to search the place. I'll get Jane started on that. Go let the team know what's happening."

Cooper left Jack and stepped into the main conference room.

Zeke immediately saw something was wrong and stood.

Sierra caught Zeke's reaction and turned. "What's going on?"

Cooper told them what he and Jack discovered. "We're heading over there now."

Cooper left to find Hannah. With Megan being pregnant, Jack wouldn't want her part of the takedown in case they ended up in a firefight with Salcedo.

He stuck his head into the small room and froze. Images of his father's embalmed victims in the cubicles his old man placed them in seemed to jump off the computer screen and mock him.

Hannah noticed his reaction and closed the laptop. "Everything okay?"

He struggled to regain his composure. "We have something." He updated both women on their findings. Cooper's attention went to Megan. "Jack told me if you tried to come with us, I was to restrain you."

Megan smiled and held up her hands. "I know my husband. I'll man the fort from here. Good luck. I hope this is our guy." Cooper did too. But could it be that simple?

"Keep me updated," Megan called after them.

As they approached the rest of the team, the weather outside seemed to have deteriorated further.

"It's getting bad," Jack confirmed. "But this can't wait. Chief Milam is having his people meet us at the house. Who wants the honor of driving in this mess?"

"I'll do it," Cooper volunteered. He needed something to distract his anxious thoughts. Jack slid into the passenger seat while Hannah got behind Cooper. Once everyone was inside, Cooper started from the portico. The parking lot was completely covered in snow. Thankfully, the Suburban was equipped with snow tires that gripped the pavement.

"According to Google, Salcedo's home is out in the middle of nowhere." Sierra had pulled up the location on her tablet. "It would certainly make the perfect place to keep his trophies."

Cooper's gaze connected with Hannah's in the rearview mirror. She'd seen his reaction to Sierra's statement. She smiled. He focused on his driving as snow continued to swirl around them. He gripped the wheel tighter when the vehicle threatened to slide a couple of times.

"The turnoff's coming up on the right." Sierra alerted him to the upcoming change of direction. "Quarter of a mile."

Cooper nodded and leaned forward, squinting through the windshield.

"Almost there."

"I see it." Cooper slowed carefully and made the turn.

"Looks like the place is about a half mile up this road. There aren't any other houses." Sierra continued to monitor the location.

Jack's cell phone rang. "It's Jane." He put the phone on speaker. "Tell me you've got the warrant."

"I do. I woke the judge up and can't say I made friends with him, but we got it." Jane laughed. "Document is on its way to you now."

"It's coming through. Thank you, Jane. Appreciate the help."

"Anytime."

"There's Chief Milam and his people." Zeke pointed to taillights that appeared through the storm.

Cooper braked harder than he expected to when the cruiser came up quickly.

Jack's phone rang again. "It's Milam." He once more placed the call on speaker. "Chief. Appreciate your assist. We have the warrant." "That's good to hear. We'll let you take the lead." "Copy you, Chief." Jack punched End.

Cooper turned off his lights and carefully passed the two cruisers. Salcedo's drive was around a curve. Cooper eased onto the driveway. "He'll know we're coming if he has any type of security at all." And if he was modeling himself to be the next Embalmer, then he'd be prepared.

Cooper parked in front of the sprawling single-story home. The two police cruisers pulled in behind them.

"We don't know what we're facing. Keep your eyes open and your weapons close." The tension in Jack's voice confirmed the seriousness of the situation.

Cooper shoved the door open and got out. Gusts of wind threatened to slam it in his face. He held it tight and shut it as quietly as possible before assisting Hannah.

"Stay close to me," he said above the wind. "I have a bad feeling." With Hannah at his side, they started for the house. Detectives Siegler and Jordan were part of Milam's team.

Jack motioned for Zeke, Sierra, and the two detectives to take the back.

Milam would accompany Jack's group.

Jack stepped up on the porch. Though it was already eight in the evening, not a single light shone inside.

"He could be gone," Hannah said.

"Possibly." Still, Cooper didn't like it.

Jack pounded on the door. "Police. Open up. We have a warrant."

The order was met with silence.

Three more attempts confirmed if Salcedo were inside, he wasn't going to let them in voluntarily.

"Tell your people to take the back."

Milam relayed the command. Jack tried the door handle. It opened freely. He stared at his team. Something bordering unease etched his face.

Cooper's internal warning bell went ballistic. Something bad was waiting for them inside. Something from his past ready to take away the house of cards he'd lived in since his mother's death.

CHAPTER TEN

"N turned to Milam. "Call them off." o—don't. It's a setup." Cooper grabbed Jack's hand then

Milam quickly gave the order. "Fall back. Could be a setup."

"You think there are explosives inside?" Jack asked once the team had moved away from the house.

"I don't know. Call it gut instinct, but something's not right."

Jack didn't question his answer. He turned to Milam. "We need a bomb squad here now."

"We don't have one on the island. I'll call in the one from Rochester. Could be a while." Milam stepped away to make the call.

"Back door was open," Zeke told them once his team joined them near the front of the house. "Something's off."

Milam returned to the group. "They're an hour out."

"Let's fall back to the road. Get these vehicles back in case the place blows," Jack gave the order.

Once the vehicles were out of danger, Cooper pulled out binoculars, switching them to night vision. Nothing moved around the house as far as he could tell. Was it all his imagination? Certainly, having the worst time in his life come back to haunt him had him on edge.

Someone touched his shoulder. He turned to find Hannah beside him. "He's watching us." His shocked eyes held hers. She pointed to the trees. "There are cameras there. Probably everywhere around the house. Inside. He was expecting us."

"You're right. I can't believe I didn't notice them." He told Jack what Hannah had discovered. "He knew we'd come here."

"Unbelievable." Jack whipped around to Zeke. "Any chance you can get us into that feed. Find out where Salcedo is hiding?"

Zeke was one of the best tech people they had on the team. "I'll try." His normal cocky assurance wasn't there, confirming the challenges.

After more than an hour of waiting, Sierra spotted the bomb squad as their headlights approached through the snowy evening. The emergency response vehicle stopped beside them, a virtual toolbox on wheels.

The window rolled down. "I'm Captain Morrison. Who's in charge?"

Jack stepped forward and identified himself. "We believe the man we're chasing rigged the house to explode when we entered." "I have video inside." Zeke came over with his laptop.

Captain Morrison got out. "Let's take a look." He motioned to his team.

Members of the unit gathered around watching the video feed from inside the house. "I see at least three explosive devices." Morrison pointed to the front entrance. "You're right. It would have detonated the second you entered the home. If he's watching, he'll try to destroy any evidence inside. Suit up, Langston, Owens. This is going to be a multi-pronged mission. We need to take out those bombs at the entrances first."

The two men prepared to put on their explosive ordnance disposal, or blast suits.

Morrison clearly had misgivings. "If he's watching as it would appear, there's a good chance he'll set off the explosives once we're close."

Jack frowned. "You think he's got the explosives tied to a cell phone he's using to monitor our movements?"

"That'd be my guess."

"What if we use a signal jammer to shut off the cameras and hopefully render him unable to explode the devices," Cooper suggested.

"It's worth a shot," Captain Morrison told them. "It will take out our ability to communicate and monitor my people's progress visually as well." "I don't think we have a choice if we want to keep your people safe. I'm calling Megan to let her know what we're doing before we lose service. I'll have her try and call back in a few minutes." Jack called his wife and explained what was happening.

Zeke waited until Jack gave the okay before initiating the signal jammer.

"Nothing here." Cooper stared at his phone. Others confirmed the same results.

Minutes went by. No calls came in.

"Looks like we're a go," Morrison told his people. "We'll have limited visual on you from here and no communication."

The two men in suits moved toward the house. Using the signal jammer had blocked all communication. The men would be on their own.

They didn't dare get any closer in case Salcedo was still able to somehow detonate the bombs.

Half an hour passed before the two entrances were free of explosives. Clearing the rest of the house took excruciatingly longer.

The two bomb squad members returned to confirm the house had been swept for further bombs and was free of danger.

"There's some strange stuff going on inside the place, though. You're going to have to see it to believe it," Langston told the group.

With the go-ahead, the vehicles were moved closer to the house. The signal jammer remained in place.

Cooper entered the house with the rest of the team.

"It's in the basement." Langston directed them downstairs.

As soon as he reached the bottom step, Cooper saw what Langston had spoken of. A man stood in front of what appeared to be a counter. Cooper drew his weapon even knowing it wouldn't be needed.

With his people backing him up, Cooper reached the propped-up man who stared straight ahead.

Cooper lowered his weapon. "That's Salcedo." The basement had been set up to resemble a pharmacy. There were shelves holding medicine containers. A measuring scale to weigh out the dosage allotted by the prescribing doctor.

"Look at his eyes." Hannah pointed to the eyes that weren't eyes at all. "Those are glass." Her gaze shot to Cooper. "Is he embalmed?"

"We'll need the medical examiner to confirm. But I'm guessing yes. My father kept his victims' eyes closed." Cooper recalled seeing photos of the embalmed victims. "This isn't sticking with my father's MO. This is something different."

"We need the medical examiner here." Jack looked to Zeke. "You'll need to turn off the signal jammer."

As soon as the jammer was turned off, service returned. Detective Jordan called the medical examiner.

"ME's on his way." Jordan shook his head. "This is stranger than anything I've seen before."

Cooper couldn't agree more.

"So Salcedo was working with the killer?" Sierra tried to make sense of it. "Did your father work with someone?"

"No, never."

"Let's search the place." Jack gave the order. "We need to identify whoever killed Salcedo and Witherspoon. He probably has Beckham. Hopefully, she's still alive."

With Hannah's help, Cooper took the basement. The rest of the team returned upstairs. Bomb squad would remain onsite in case there were any unforeseen problems.

Hannah opened one of the pill containers. "There are pills in here. They look real."

Cooper came over and peered over her shoulder. "You're right." He opened several other containers with the same results. "What was Salcedo doing with this kind of medication?"

"Maybe selling it?" Hannah searched through some paperwork lying on the counter beside him. "Names. This is going to be more involved than we thought. We need ERT here now."

"You're right. Let's try not to disturb anything further. I'll call ERT."

Returning upstairs, Cooper called Bob Foster, the lead technician for the FBI's Evidence Recovery Team.

Bob greeted him as a friend. Working cases together had created a bond Cooper was grateful for. Bob was about the same age as his father would have been yet nothing like the monster hidden beneath Oliver Ellison's polished exterior.

"Let me guess, you need my team there now?"

Cooper chuckled at Bob's uncanny ability to read the truth from a few simple words. "We do." He explained what they'd found. "This is way beyond anything we've encountered before."

"I'll call my people. We can be there in an hour."

"Thanks, Bob." Cooper ended the call.

Hannah had already told Jack what they'd discovered in the basement.

"We need to dig into Salcedo. If he has that much medication at his house, I want to know how he got away with stealing it without anyone knowing."

"I'll see what I can find." Cooper went outside to retrieve his laptop.

When the medical examiner and his team arrived, Cooper explained what they believed had been done to Salcedo.

"I remember the original Embalmer case," Doctor Tinner told him. Cooper braced for what would come. Most of the time, he went unrecognized whenever someone spoke about his father's case . . . but not always.

"Once we get the body to the lab, we'll be able to tell more about the technique used to embalm our victim."

A thorough search of the house didn't divulge any hint at who Salcedo might've been working with. The aspect of selling drugs was probably something Salcedo did on his own, but they couldn't afford to dismiss that whoever killed him might have been part of it.

CHAPTER ELEVEN

The video of the house came back online, but it was too late. They'd defused his little presents and had searched the entire house.

"You shouldn't have placed the bombs there. What if they trace them back to you?" Mentor's anger seared through his brain. He'd messed up. Wanted to do something on his own to impress his mentor and failed miserably as always.

"I'm sorry. You're right." But he didn't regret what he'd done to Salcedo, family or not. He deserved everything he got. He'd gone off script by selling those prescription drugs to thugs. He'd put everything at risk.

"Did you leave anything that can be traced back to us?" Mentor's displeasure was clear in the succinct way he spoke.

He thought carefully. He'd worked hard to gain Mentor's respect. He couldn't fail him.

"No, nothing."

"Not even the explosives?" The question reverberated in his head.

He'd been careful. Used items from his home that could be bought anywhere. There would be no tracing it to him. "No, not even the explosives."

Mentor wasn't convinced. "It's time for our next immortal."

He whirled toward Mentor. "I thought *she* was next." He'd picked out the perfect woman to be part of their family.

"You're not ready to pick yet. I have someone in mind." Mentor stared at the screen as they watched the federal agents and other law enforcement agents combing through Salcedo's home.

"Who is she?" He had to admit, the thought of searching for his next family member was exciting. The woman he'd found would be perfect despite Mentor's objection. She was smart and pretty like Tiffany. He regretted not being able to spend more time with Tiffany. He'd enjoyed their chats. Perhaps he'd be allowed to keep the next beauty longer. Perhaps he wouldn't listen to Mentor's incessant jabbering.

"I have chosen the perfect one. A doctor." Mentor's voice softened. "She will make a wonderful addition to our family. She's clever and intelligent. This will be your greatest challenge. We'll see if you are worthy to be my apprentice after the way you messed up with my ballerina." Mentor smiled nastily.

Soon, Mentor lost interest, probably reliving his glory days.

Now was the perfect time to watch the one *he* had chosen. She would prove challenging, but he'd fought too hard to get to this point. He wouldn't let Mentor change his mind.

He smiled at her pretty face. Flawless caramel-colored skin. Raven hair. Almond eyes. Breathtaking. Much better than Mentor's choice, whom he felt no connection to at all.

His chosen one was responsible for deciding the guilty and the innocent, much like he did. He thought about the stimulating conversations they'd have before she became immortal.

◆◆◆

Hannah stared up at the sky as the weather continued to deteriorate with the fading day. ERT had arrived shortly after the medical examiner left with Harold Salcedo's body.

"We might as well return to the hotel and get some rest," Jack told his team. "It will be hours before ERT has any answers, and I have a feeling this is going to be a long process to unravel what's really going on here."

Hannah claimed her place behind Cooper in the SUV. She closed her eyes. The endless hours were taking their toll. She grabbed her water and as discreetly as possible took her medicine. When she looked up, she noticed Cooper watching her in the rearview mirror. Like it or not, she'd have to tell him the truth soon.

Once they arrived at the hotel, Hannah gathered her bag and room key and prepared to go to her room until Jack asked to speak to her before she headed upstairs. She dreaded what would come.

"Everything okay?" Cooper asked when he noticed the exchange. "You don't look so good."

Hannah flinched at his unknowing insult. "I'm fine. You should get some sleep."

"I don't think I can. Too much going round in my head. If you want to talk once you're finished with the boss, I'm in 208."

She forced a smile and watched him leave before finding Jack and Megan in one of the smaller conference rooms.

"I'm okay," she said as soon as she'd entered the room.

Both Jack and Megan looked up.

"Are you sure?" Megan obviously had seen what Cooper had.

"I'm positive. I'm pacing myself. I'm taking my meds. I'm okay."

Megan glanced to her husband. "We're only concerned about your health, Hannah. You told us how hard it was when Ellie died. And you just got over the flu."

"I realize that, but I'm doing better. Today hasn't been all that stressful." Not exactly the truth but she wouldn't tell them the exhaustion that weighed down her limbs.

Megan touched her arm. "Promise you'll let us know if you need a break. You are too important as a friend and to the team to let anything happen to you."

Hannah smiled. "Thank you. And I promise I will." She gave both her friends a hug and then left.

Once she reached her room, Hannah placed her bag on the bed and sat down beside it. She checked her phone again. No further disturbances at her home. She typed a short message to her neighbor to check on the place as soon as possible then grabbed her nightgown and showered.

The warmth of the water eased some of the weariness from her body. She couldn't get the case out of her head. How was Salcedo involved? Obviously, there was someone else calling the shots.

Her phone beeped. Bert.

Checked the house. No signs of anyone tampering with the place. I saw the rock you mentioned. Strange. Looks like you may have a secret admirer. Probably some neighborhood kid.

If only it were so.

She thanked him.

You have my heart.

She could almost dismiss the earlier note left on her kitchen table. But this. There was no denying someone who knew about her transplant was targeting her.

Hannah stretched out on the bed and closed her eyes. Rest would put some of her anxieties at ease.

◆◆◆

He'd broken her nose. Broken bones in her hand when she'd dared try to defend herself. As she stared at the bloodied woman in the mirror, one truth became clear. He'd eventually kill her. Each time he beat her, he swore he'd change. But he hadn't. Whenever she did something to set him off, she watched as the monster took over and the sweet man she'd married disappeared. It was as if with each beating her sweetheart was vanishing a little more, and the monster was claiming more control.

She couldn't turn to her family. She'd put them in danger by doing so. Her friend from the church helped her, but she was almost certain the monster had followed them. He'd never mentioned it, but she was sure he'd been there. If so, then her friend would suffer her fate. She couldn't let that happen. But could she do what must be done? She touched her broken face, tears streaming down from her eyes. Could she stand up to the monster once and for all and bring him down?

◆◆◆

Hannah's eyes shot open. Tears soaking her face. She knew it was just a dream, and yet she couldn't help it. Hannah went to the mirror. No bruises. No swollen face. Just the hauntings of a nightmare she didn't understand.

Suddenly, the walls closed in and the thought of being alone rehashing that dream didn't appeal. If she reached out to Zeke, he'd have a million questions she didn't want to answer.

Hannah scrolled to Cooper's number.

Want to get something to eat?

The hotel had a small restaurant inside. Hopefully, it would still be open. She dressed quickly and did her best to remove all traces of her tears when a knock at her door had her smiling. She crossed the room and opened it to find Cooper waiting.

"Couldn't sleep?" he asked.

"Not really. Too much going on in my head." Not exactly the truth. Hannah grabbed her bag and key card, and they started down the stairs.

"I get that." He tried the restaurant door. It opened freely. Cooper held it for her.

Hannah was happy to see none of her team was dining.

The hostess came to seat them. "The storm has diminished our kitchen staff, but we will try and accommodate your choices."

"Thanks." Hannah picked up her menu. She could feel Cooper's eyes on her. She didn't want to do it. Yet she owed it to him.

In the end she ordered a salad while Cooper settled for a burger and fries so loaded with grease that it would make her doctor cringe.

He glanced around the restaurant before homing in on her. "What's going on, Hannah? Why the sudden change toward me? And don't tell me it's my imagination, because I know it isn't."

She sipped her water and tried to find the right words.

The strain on her face must have grabbed his attention. "Hannah? What is it?" he prompted when she still hesitated.

She blew out a weary sigh. "I've never told anyone this before. Megan and Jack know because, well, they came to my house and saw how sick I was."

Cooper gripped his glass tight. "You had the flu."

She shook her head. "It's more than that. Something happened to me when I was twelve."

"You're scaring me," he said. "Just tell me."

Hannah swallowed and then laid it out for him. "I had a heart transplant." She chanced a quick look his way, but Cooper seemed incapable of speaking for a second.

"Y-you had a heart transplant? Why didn't you tell me before now? We were close. We . . ." The pain in his voice confirmed she'd hurt him again. Truth be told, she'd hurt a lot of people.

She hadn't told him before because she didn't want to have him look at her the way he was right now. Or have him treat her differently.

"I'd been sick most of my life. My heart just gave out when I was twelve. I was rushed to the hospital and remained in a coma until a donor was found."

Cooper couldn't seem to grasp what she said. "We shared so much about our lives and our pasts. You should have told me about this."

"Why? You didn't tell me about your father."

"That's different." He bit back the rest of what he'd been about to say when the waitress brought their food.

"How?" she asked once the waitress was out of earshot. "You lived through something you didn't want anyone to know about. *You* didn't want to be judged by your past. How is it different?"

He appeared to struggle to gain control over his anger.

She leaned forward. "I didn't tell you because it was a part of my life I wanted to forget. Do you have any idea how hard it was growing up and knowing I was different from the other kids? My own mother used work to distance herself."

His expression softened, and he reached for her hand. "Hannah."

Hannah's mouth twisted bitterly. "She believed God was punishing her for something. She never said what. Anyway, she kind of checked out of my life after the transplant. My father left when I was still in the hospital because he couldn't deal with the strict regimen that I'd have to adhere to for the rest of my life."

"I'm so sorry, Hannah. I've no right to judge you. You're right. I didn't share things with you either."

She smiled sadly. "I guess we both kept secrets."

"But what does what happened to you in the past have to do with us?" He didn't understand. That made her sadder.

She tried to pull her hand free.

"No, Hannah. Don't. Tell me. There's something else, isn't there?"

"Yes, there is. I was sick with the flu recently, but I also lost my friend." Her voice broke. Just talking about Ellie's death reminded Hannah that she'd lost one of her biggest allies.

"She and I met in a support group for transplant patients. We were both young when we received our hearts. We practically grew up together." "What happened to her?" he asked, his attention on her face.

"Her heart happened to her. She developed an infection, and they couldn't control it. She died a week after being admitted to the hospital. I didn't even get to say goodbye."

Hannah fought back tears. She didn't realize Cooper had claimed the seat beside her until he tugged her into his arms and leaned his head against hers. "I'm so sorry. That must have been heartbreaking."

Just for a moment, she let herself be comforted by him then she pulled away and scrubbed her hands over her cheeks.

"Cooper, the average lifespan of a transplant patient is a little under ten years. Ellie lost her battle at seventeen." She turned her head his way. "I've had my transplant for nineteen years."

He tried to hide his reaction and couldn't. "But that doesn't have to be you, Hannah."

She couldn't let him continue. "There's a very real chance it will be. I have to be realistic, Cooper. I could die." She choked the words out. "Zeke is family. I can't ask anyone else to go through this with me."

"You can't shut your life off like that. You aren't living it to the fullest if you do. I care about you, Hannah. I-l—"

She couldn't let him say the words. "I'm sorry, Cooper. I just can't. I care about you as well. Too much to let you watch me die." She touched his face, wishing for. . . "It wouldn't work. Don't you see? We'd constantly be expecting the end. You'd regret your decision soon, and so would I. We can be friends. I want that, I need you in my life. But you have to let *us* go. We can't be, Cooper. Get on with your life. Be happy. Don't let your father's sins become yours. Fall in love."

He slowly rose. "I already have. I love you, Hannah. I'll always love you. Only you. But I can't make it work between us by myself. It's up to you. If you change your mind, you let me know." And just like that, with those words ringing in her ears, Cooper left her alone with the heartbreaking truth.

He loved her.

CHAPTER TWELVE

"Sdeep concentration.

he's not the right one." Mentor's angry voice penetrated his

"She is right. You'll see."

The chilly silence that followed proved Mentor didn't agree.

Sitting in the car, he watched and waited for the lights to extinguish. Judge Veronica Turner had a stellar record on the bench. She'd risen through the ranks going from clerking for a judge to having her own gavel by the age of twenty-eight. One of the few African American judges in the county, she dedicated herself to being a fair judge. And because of it, she'd gained celebrity status. Her face had been on the cover of dozens of national magazines. The up-and-coming face of the judicial future.

And she would be the perfect addition to rest eternally alongside Tiffany and the others to come.

Excitement coursed through his veins.

"You have the syringe?" Mentor barked out the question. Mentor's stern tone pulled him back to earth.

He patted his pocket. "I do and an extra one in case. I'm all set."

"You will have to pull the car up around back, but first kill the security feed. If they catch a glimpse of you everything will fall apart."

He tamped down his anger. "Yes, I know." He'd watched his mentor when he first killed. Learned from everything he said. He knew what he was doing.

The living room light went out. He leaned forward in anticipation, watching as first the kitchen light then the other lights in the house disappeared.

Minutes ticked by while the exhilaration grew inside him.

"It's time."

His jaw set. "I can see that." The words snapped from his lips as he got out. He could feel Mentor's displeasure following him as he eased close enough for the program to activate on his tablet.

Soon, the security system turned off. She would have no idea she slept unprotected.

This was the part he loved the most. Slipping inside the house. Touching things that she had touched. Her perfume lingering in the air. Seeing her sleeping peacefully in her bed unaware eternity was so close.

In the living room, she'd left work lying on the coffee table. He sat and picked up one of the documents, holding it close to make out the words. A case of a teenage girl who had been raped by a football player. The type of case that would be right up her alley. Veronica was a champion of the underdog.

He could almost feel Mentor's disdain at how long he was taking. A slow smile spread across his face. Good. He wouldn't rush this part. It was his favorite.

In the kitchen she'd left a glass of wine half-finished on the island. One of the things he'd admired about her was how she had control over her faculties. Veronica never once got drunk in public. Not like Giselle.

He lifted the glass to sniff the wine. Sweet. Perfect for her.

It was time. He eased toward the bedroom where he knew she would be sleeping by now because he'd watched her sleep before.

The door stood ajar. She left it that way because she owned a cat. A furry little tabby who was pictured in photos around the house.

The cat meowed before jumping from the bed. Veronica moaned and turned on her side without waking.

He removed the syringe from his pocket. Veronica was fit and a blackbelt in martial arts. Mentor had trained him well. Act quickly. Get her disabled and then remove her from her home. Once she was under his control and safely in her final resting place, he'd enjoy her company before she became immortal.

Mentor told him never to deviate from his instructions. They'd been drilled into him from a young age.

What did it hurt to enjoy a few more moments to watch her sleep? She would be even more special than Tiffany. He wanted to spend more time with Veronica. Get to know her beyond the facts he'd read.

He sat down on the bed, careful not to wake her. More than the ten minutes Mentor demanded he adhere to had passed. Once he returned, there would be the wrath of Mentor to deal with, but he didn't care.

He reached up and touched her hair. So glossy. Her skin flawless. Not a single blemish. Tiffany had been close to perfect, but Veronica . . .

Her eyes shot open. Surprise turned to horror, and her mouth opened to scream.

No, no, no.

He clamped his hand over her mouth, stifling the scream. He jabbed the syringe into her neck.

She shoved him hard. The force took him by surprise. He lost his balance and tumbled to the floor then jumped quickly to his feet.

Veronica opened the drawer of her nightstand. She had a gun.

Why wasn't the medicine working?

He retrieved the second syringe from his pocket. An angry growl escaped as he lunged for her, the syringe pointed like a weapon. He hit her before she grabbed the weapon. He jabbed the second needle into her neck near the first injection.

She didn't go down easily. Veronica continued to fight him with everything she had until the medicine took hold and she relaxed her grip on him as she lost consciousness.

He lowered her onto the bed, struggling to get his breath back. She had proven a formidable opponent. He looked forward to more challenges during their time together.

CHAPTER   THIRTEEN

"Y one of the carafes the hotel supplied in the conference room ou look terrible. Couldn't sleep?" Zeke poured coffee from where they were meeting.

Cooper chose to take out his frustration on his friend. "Hannah told me everything. About her transplant."

Zeke whipped his way. "She told you?" The shock on Zeke's face confirmed Cooper hadn't imagined the devastating news delivered by Hannah.

"She did. Finally. You should have." Cooper bit the words out.

Zeke motioned him away from the team members who were gathered near the window.

Cooper followed, regretting his outburst. Zeke was a good friend and had his back through numerous cases.

"I couldn't. I wanted to tell you, but it wasn't my place, Cooper. You see that, don't you?"

Cooper blew out a breath. "You're right. It just took me by surprise."

Zeke searched his face. "What did she say?"

"Only that she hoped we could be friends." The words came out reflecting the bitterness in his heart.

"Oh, man, I'm sorry, Coop. I know how you feel about her." Zeke glanced to his coffee cup. "She's scared. Her friend died. Hannah's convinced her life has a timetable on it—which the ugly truth is, she's right."

Cooper's heart felt as if it were wrenched from his body. He'd heard the words. Listened to Hannah as she told him about her friend's recent death, and yet he couldn't equate that tragedy with Hannah.

"I won't accept that." For all his bravado he couldn't stop the inevitable. When it was Hannah's time to leave this earth, short of another transplant, she would be in God's hands.

Zeke glanced past him to the door. Cooper turned as Hannah entered the room.

She looked like she'd gotten about as much sleep as he did.

Jack called them over. "Let's get started. Where are we so far? Cooper, what do we know about Salcedo?"

Cooper had given up on sleep and dug into Harold Salcedo more deeply. "He was fired from the last two pharmacies. There were accusations of missing drugs though the businesses couldn't prove it was Salcedo."

"Any known associates?"

Cooper shook his head. "I checked. He appeared to be a bit of a loner. I'm guessing that was purposeful. Easier to commit a crime when there's no one hanging around."

"I read through the fan letters sent to your father," Sierra told him. "There are some sick women out there. Again, the women have all been cleared. Still, what makes someone want to write to a serial killer?"

Cooper had no idea. "What about the doctor who treated my dad in prison?"

"Oh, I have this one." Megan clicked some keys on her laptop. "She no longer works there. She left a few weeks after your father died."

"Any idea where she's living now?" Cooper wanted to speak to her as soon as possible.

Megan nodded. "She has a cabin in the woods about two hours from here."

Cooper rose and grabbed his coat. "Feel like a ride?" he asked Zeke.

"Let's go." Zeke finished his coffee.

"I'll send you the directions." Megan confirmed with Zeke.

"I'm coming with you." Hannah stood.

He cringed. Their conversation the night before still ripped at his heart. But that wasn't all. With the reality of her condition staring him in the face, Cooper didn't want anything to happen to her. No matter how angry he was with the way she'd handled things, he didn't want to lose her to the job. To this killer.

She stood with her hands on her hips. "The doctor is female. She might not be willing to talk to you guys."

"She has a point." Zeke came to the defense of his sister.

"Alright." Cooper had no right to tell her what to do. She'd told him Jack and Megan knew about her illness and had okayed her to work.

He held the door open for her. She passed by, glaring at him as she did.

Zeke followed his sister, giving Cooper a pat on the back. It was going to be a strained two-hour-long trip if he didn't get a handle on his anger.

He waited while Hannah bundled up. The storm hadn't been as bad as they expected. Yet another one was moving in that was predicted to be far worse.

Cooper got behind the wheel, surprised that Hannah slipped into the passenger seat beside him. Maybe that was a good sign.

He turned onto the main road leading from the island and glanced in the rearview. "You have the address?" he asked Zeke.

"I do. She's outside of Syracuse." Zeke gave directions to Interstate 90.

The roads had been graded since the storm and were relatively free of ice and debris.

"This is odd."

He shifted his attention to Hannah, who studied her tablet. "Did you find out something on the doctor?"

"I did. Isobel Melendez appears to have disappeared off the face of the earth."

Cooper frowned, not following her. "What do you mean?"

"There are no credit card transactions in years. No social media."

"Maybe she went off grid." Zeke said. "According to Google Maps, her house is in the middle of the woods. It stands to reason after working for a prison for what—eight years—she'd seen the worst in humanity. Some people can't handle that."

"You think she flipped out and moved to the woods to get away from what she'd seen?" Cooper was skeptical.

"It's possible. People check out for far less reasons."

He thought about Hannah. She hadn't checked out entirely, but losing her friend had certainly put up her guard. Hannah caught him looking, and he focused on the road ahead. He couldn't imagine how frightening it must have been hearing her friend, who had her heart for less time than Hannah, was gone.

Cooper's phone interrupted his troubled thoughts. Jack's number popped on the screen. He answered the call and put it on speaker. "Anything wrong?"

"Possibly. A county judge was just reported missing from her home." Jack gave the judge's name.

Immediately, a pit formed in Cooper's stomach. "You think this is our guy?"

"We can't afford to dismiss it. Her security system was dismantled like Beckham's and Witherspoon's. We're meeting the detectives over at her place. We'll keep you posted."

Zeke blew out a whistle. "Veronica Turner is one impressive judge." He leaned forward to show both Hannah and Cooper the judge's photo. "Definitely on her way up the ladder."

"We should check into her cases." Hannah shrugged when Cooper arched a brow. "Her disappearance probably isn't connected to her job, but we can't dismiss anything." She typed on her tablet. "And as he's proven, our copycat doesn't seem to have any qualms about taking high-profile victims."

"He's confident." Cooper tasted the bitterness in his mouth. Just like his old man. Cooper had always admired that about his father. He'd told his son that he could accomplish anything in life if he believed in himself.

How had that man—the one Cooper thought hung the moon—turned into a monster? Even counseling hadn't helped him understand this, but he'd learned to accept it and move on.

"He's escalating," Hannah said. "Your father usually took his victims months apart. Our copycat is deviating from that MO."

Which meant, who knew what he would throw at them next?

"Road to Melendez's place is up ahead on the left."

"Thanks, Zeke." Cooper spotted the road and turned. As soon as he saw the condition of it, he stopped and wondered if Zeke had it right. "You sure about this?"

It was a dirt road that looked slicker than all get out.

"According to our records."

Cooper put the Suburban into four-wheel drive to keep from slipping into the ditch. "I've got a bad feeling about this one."

He slowed the vehicle's speed to a crawl. The sky above became dark and threatening. Fitting for their purpose here. "When's that storm supposed to hit?" he asked uneasily.

"Weather report said this afternoon. I think they got it wrong." Zeke showed them the winter cold front moving in on his screen. "Looks like we're in for a far worse one than yesterday. They're calling for blizzard conditions."

"Great." Cooper continued along the road. "How much farther?"

Zeke checked the screen. "You're almost on top of her drive." He leaned close to the window. "There."

Cooper braked when he realized he'd passed it. He eased the SUV back until he could safely make the turn. "Let's stay alert." Once more his earlier fears came back to haunt him. Had he put Hannah in jeopardy by agreeing to her coming?

Like you could stop her.

The drive appeared to be little more than a trail that stopped abruptly in front of a tiny cabin.

"Wait, she went from being a doctor at a prison to living here?" Zeke exclaimed, clearly surprised by the change.

"Apparently so." Cooper slid the SUV into Park. "I don't see any lights on inside." His bad feeling doubled at the sight of the cabin. "Keep your weapons close." He wanted to tell Hannah to stay behind, but he had no right.

Cooper got out and was joined by Hannah and Zeke.

He glanced around half expecting an ambush. When they stepped up on the porch, Cooper eased to the window and peeked inside. A small living room, with dining and kitchen beyond. The house was dark. No sign of the doctor.

Zeke rapped on the door. Silence followed the sound.

"Doctor Melendez. Federal agents." Hannah called out. "Open up."

The request was met with more silence.

"We don't have a warrant to search the place. Let's check around back." Cooper stepped from the porch and headed to the side of the cabin. Hannah followed him.

Zeke took the opposite side.

"There's a barn back here." Cooper pointed to a structure that was mostly disguised by overgrown trees.

Hannah grabbed his arm. "I see a light beneath the door."

Cooper spotted it, too. From the opposite side of the house, Zeke converged on their location.

As they approached, what sounded like a radio could be heard. "Someone's in there." Cooper's grip tightened on his Glock when the door opened, and a woman emerged. She carried a bag in one hand and a shotgun in the other.

She spotted them and dropped the bag, wielding the shotgun in front of her as if she'd been expecting trouble. "Who are you? Why are you on my property?"

"We're FBI agents," Cooper told her. "I'm reaching for my ID." He showed her the FBI credentials. "Are you Doctor Melendez?"

Her surprise was clear. "Not anymore. It's just Isobel Melendez now. I gave up practicing medicine."

The more Cooper learned about Melendez, the harder it was to get a read on her.

"What do you want?" She clearly didn't want to have a conversation with them. Her anger at their intrusion into her life showed on her face.

"To talk. Only to talk. Can you please lower your weapon." Cooper kept a careful watch on the shotgun. From the way she held it, she'd be skilled at using it when necessary. Did she have it for protection from wild animals that she might come across . . . or from danger coming from a twolegged predator?

She slowly lowered the gun. Her eyes locked onto Cooper and then she appeared to recognize him. "Wait—do I know you?"

They'd never met. There could be only one way she would.

"You're Oliver's son."

She'd treated his old man. Chances are Cooper had come up in their conversations. But Cooper hadn't once visited the prison.

"You look a lot like him. I heard you became an FBI agent."

It was his turn to be surprised. "What do you mean you heard? My father's been dead for years. You would have no reason to keep tabs on me." Cooper forgot about Hannah and Zeke. Something was terribly wrong.

Isobel Melendez slowly smiled. "You're right. Except I promised your dad I'd watch out for you." Her smile disappeared. "Back then, he could be quite persuasive."

After his father's capture, Cooper had been questioned about other women. What did he know about Oliver's relationship with the women he'd killed. Cooper had no idea if his father had cheated on his mother.

"It's getting colder out here. Do you mind if we come inside and ask you some questions?"

Melendez didn't seem eager to have that part of her life brought up.

"There's been another woman killed recently." Cooper watched her face. She didn't seem surprised. "If you know something that might help us stop the person copycatting my father's crimes you need to tell us." When she remained silent, he added, "Two women are missing as well. One just last night. A judge. He won't keep her alive long."

Melendez blew out a sigh. "I can't believe this is happening. I thought . . ." She eyed them all. "Alright. Come inside." She shouldered past Cooper and headed toward the house. Cooper saw the same surprise on Hannah's and Zeke's faces as he wore.

The door stood open. Cooper stepped into the kitchen. Zeke closed the door behind him and Hannah.

Melendez stood in the living room looking out at their vehicle. "I should have known I couldn't escape this. I left my job and everything to come here to escape your father's crimes."

Hannah went over to her. "I'm sorry you went through that. Did you love him?"

Melendez's eyes grew large. Tears were there in the depths of her pain. "In the beginning."

Cooper and Zeke hung back to let Hannah conduct the interview. As a profiler, she had skills that saw human characteristics most people didn't. She'd seen the truth about Melendez's relationship with his dad.

"How did it start?" Hannah's gentle question encouraged her to open up. There was no judgment in her tone. Only sympathy.

"Little by little." Melendez laughed. "Like it always does. Of course, I knew who he was. In fact, I had misgivings about treating him. I expected a monster. Oliver wasn't one . . . at least not in the beginning."

Cooper thought about the man he knew. Nothing about his father had prepared him for learning his dad was a serial killer.

"We talked about family. He spoke about you often." She shifted her attention to Cooper. "My boy this, and my boy that." Melendez shook her head. "Getting to know him, I believed him when he told me he'd been set up to take the fall for someone else."

This grabbed Cooper's attention. "He told you he'd been set up?" A glimmer of hope chiseled through the place where he'd buried his feelings for his father. Cooper tamped it back down. It was a lie. His father had played this woman just as he had all the others. If he'd been able to find a way, his dad would have claimed her as his victim as well.

"He talked about that all the time. I believed him." She glanced out the window, embarrassed. "We grew closer. I made up reasons to have him come to the infirmary. We fell in love . . . or rather, I fell in love. He was using me."

"How was he using you, Isobel?" Hannah's question brought Melendez's attention back to her. "He had you delivering messages to people, didn't he?"

"How did you know?" Isobel appeared surprised she'd guessed the truth.

"You loved him. You wanted to make him happy. He trusted you." Hannah shrugged.

"I did love him." Melendez wiped her hand across her face.

"Who did you deliver the notes to, Isobel?" Hannah pressed her. "Were they the women who visited him in prison? The men?"

Melendez hesitated.

"Please, we need your help. It's possible whoever received those notes might have been involved in Ellison's crimes. He could be the one responsible for the murders now."

"It wasn't anyone who visited him. I think Oliver used him as cover. He was close to Oliver's age, I believe, and he gave me the creeps."

They had something. Finally, they had something. "What's his name?" Cooper asked.

Isobel turned his way with a look of fear written on her face. "I don't know. Oliver never told me."

"He had to call him something?" Cooper pressed on. They needed a name.

"He did. He called him brother."

CHAPTER FOURTEEN

"**B**father didn't have any siblings.

rother?" The word tore from Cooper. Not possible. Cooper's

"That's what he called him," Melendez told him.

"Where did you meet this man to deliver the messages?" Hannah studied Isobel's reaction to each question. She was clearly frightened of the man Oliver claimed as his brother.

"At a shopping center about ten miles from the prison. I-I hated those meetings, and I told Oliver as much. He knew the man gave me the creeps, but he claimed it was important."

"How did you know where to meet this man?" Cooper asked.

Isobel told them Oliver gave her a cell number to call. "I got brave once and tried the number again after Oliver died. The message said no longer in service. It was probably a disposable phone." She gave Hannah the number, but Hannah didn't believe they'd have any luck tracking the mysterious brother after so long.

From everything Hannah had read about Ellison, he was a master manipulator. "Did you ever peek at one of those notes?" Right away, Hannah could tell she had.

"Once. It was weird. It said, 'It's time for me to take over for you. I trained you well. Soon, we will be together, and we will be unstoppable.'"

"Wait, was he planning on breaking out?" Hannah waited for an answer.

Isobel looked down at her hands. "I don't know. Possibly. He told me one day he and I would be together too . . . and then he got killed."

"He was shanked by another patient while coming to his appointment at the infirmary."

She nodded. "That's right. The shiv hit his heart. It was over before I could do anything."

Hannah sensed there was something important Isobel hadn't told them.

"Anyway, after his death I spotted someone following me one day. It was the same man I'd met. I-I was terrified. If he was carrying on Oliver's work, then had he targeted me for death?"

"Is that why you left the prison?" Hannah asked.

Isobel finally looked at her. "Yes. I moved away. I lived in fear for years." Her eyes bored into Hannah's "What if you've brought him to me? What if he finds me again because of you?"

"We can protect you," Zeke assured her. "I'll call the local police and have them sit on your house until we catch this man."

Isobel appeared relieved. "Thank you. I've lived through years of nightmares. I finally began to relax. I can't go through that again."

Hannah placed her hand on Isobel's arm. "You'll be okay. We can have people stationed around the house." She looked to Zeke, who confirmed with a nod and grabbed his phone. "We'll stay with you until they arrive." She hesitated. "Do you remember anything Oliver might have said that will help us identify this person you met with?"

Isobel clearly did.

"You can trust us," Hannah confirmed. "I promise you can."

Isobel slowly nodded. "Wait here." She hurried down the hall.

"PD is on their way. They'll have two patrols on the place at all times." Zeke returned his phone to his pocket then turned to Cooper. "Maybe this guy is family. You ever hear your old man talk about them before?"

"Talk about them—I knew them. His parents lived outside Rochester on a farm. We were over there all the time until they both passed away

within five years of each other. He never mentioned any other family.”
Cooper frowned.

Isobel returned carrying a small sketchbook. She handed it to
Hannah. “He gave me this. They’re drawings. Oliver was very talented.”
Hannah opened the book. The first sketch was of Isobel. “You’re right, he
was gifted.” She showed Cooper. “Did you know?”

Cooper smiled. “I did. He was always sketching something. Usually
my mother. Sometimes me. When we went on fishing trips, he’d sketch our
surroundings.”

“He told me,” Isobel said. “There are some sketches of you, Cooper,
and I’m guessing your mother . . . and other women.”

Hannah flipped to the first woman while Cooper looked over her
shoulder. “That’s my mother.” He said with a catch in his voice.

She touched his arm before she kept going. “Is this you?” A younger
version of Cooper smiled at the artist.

He laughed. “Yeah. I must have been around ten then.”

“Are these your grandparents?” Zeke pointed to a sketch of a couple.

Cooper studied the drawing. “That’s not them. I don’t know who
these people are.”

“Are you sure?” Isobel asked. “He told me this drawing was of his
parents.”

“He lied.” Cooper ground out the words. Just like he’d lied about
everything.

Then came sketches of Ellison’s victims. Hannah recognized them
all. And on the last pages of the sketchbook, he’d drawn a man. The
resemblance to Ellison was uncanny. She turned the page toward Isobel. “Is
this the man you met with?”

“Yes, that’s him.” Isobel appeared visibly shaken. “His eyes. I’ll
never forget his eyes.”

Hannah focused on them and saw the reason for Isobel’s fear. They
were deep holes lacking in any emotion. No expression showed on his face.
Something was written in the corner of the drawing. “What’s this?”
Hannah squinted to make out two letters. P.A. “Those must be his initials.”
It wasn’t much, but it might help them narrow down the identity of
Ellison’s brother.

"Your grandparents never mentioned having another son?" Zeke asked Cooper.

"Never." But then, the people he'd told Isobel were his parents were not.

"Did your family always live in Rochester?" Hannah asked, and he saw where she was going with the questioning.

"They lived in Pennsylvania before moving to Rochester," Cooper said with a hard edge to his voice. "Dad never liked to talk about his life back then. It was almost as if it didn't really start until Rochester."

"Maybe it was because he had to leave whoever this person is behind. He would naturally feel guilty about that. Perhaps they reconnected later."

Cooper's mouth turned up into a bitter smile. "And they realized they had a common hobby. They both loved to kill?" Outside two patrol vehicles eased up the drive.

"I'll speak to them." Zeke stepped outside.

"Do you remember anything else?" Hannah asked Isobel.

She ran a hand across her eyes. "Not really. I'm sorry. Oliver asked me to watch out for his son." She looked to Cooper once more. "I thought he was being a caring dad, but after . . . well, I wondered if he wasn't manipulating me in some way."

"What did you tell him about me?" Cooper asked in a clipped tone.

"Not much. By then I'd started to have doubts about his feelings for me even though I still loved him." She sighed. "So I gave him some little things to make him think I was cooperating. I found out you were adopted by an older couple. I never gave him their last name or where they lived." She smiled at Cooper. "For what it's worth, I really believe he loved you."

Cooper didn't respond.

Zeke returned to the house with one of the officers. "This is Patrick Redding." He introduced the officer to Isobel. "He and his people will take care of you."

"We'll be stationed all around your home, ma'am. Don't worry about a thing."

Isobel sighed in relief. "I appreciate that."

"Here's my card." Hannah gave her the card with her number on it. "If you need anything or if you remember anything, reach out anytime."

Hannah hoped that after today, they'd earned some of Isobel's respect because she couldn't help but believe there was something the former doctor hadn't told them.

"I will. Catch him. Please. I haven't really had a good night's sleep in years."

Outside, the snow started falling as they left Isobel's property.

"She's terrified." Hannah glanced back at the house. "She uprooted her life because she was scared of this man."

"If this is my father's brother and he's carrying on his crimes, finding him won't be easy. So far, there have been no fingerprints left behind. And the initials P.A. seem to indicate he had a different last name."

"Maybe your father changed his name to put the past behind him. I'll see what Jane can find out for us," Zeke said and called their office manager.

"How are you holding up with all of this?" Hannah asked while Zeke spoke to Jane. Despite the way things had ended between them the previous evening she still cared about Cooper.

"I'm numb." He glanced her way. "I thought my father's poison had ended with his death. Now, I see he's still hurting people from the grave." Hannah's cell phone rang as Zeke ended the call with Jane. "It's Jack." She placed the call on speaker for them to hear. "How goes the search for the judge?"

"Not well. There's some sign of a struggle. A lamp turned over in the bedroom. Chairs displaced. She appears to have fought her attacker much like Giselle. Unlike Giselle, she's missing. If this is the copycat, then Veronica has been deemed worthy." The frustration in Jack's tone came through clearly. "Both the judge's parents are dead. She has a sister who is on her way over here now to tell us if anything is missing. Did you find out anything useful from the doctor?"

"We did." Hannah's attention went to the sketchbook as she told Jack about their meeting with Isobel.

"So, there's a possible brother involved."

"Yes. She met with him a few times. Said he gave her the creeps." Hannah looked over at Cooper, whose jaw ticked. "We're on our way back to the hotel now. Do you want us to detour to the judge's home to assist?"

"No, we've got it covered here. Get started on finding the brother. We really need something to break our way."

CHAPTER FIFTEEN

He sat next to her bed soaking in her beauty as he waited for her to awake.

"You shouldn't have dosed her so much." Mentor had been displeased when he told him about the struggle. "You could have killed her."

"I knew what I was doing." He snapped to shut Mentor up. Mentor's surprise quickly turned to anger, which he ignored.

He turned back to her and smiled. She would wake soon. He'd checked Veronica's pulse. Weak but steady.

"I told you she was all wrong." Mentor stood behind him silently judging. It didn't matter. Soon, Mentor's help would no longer be needed. Soon, it would be just him to carry on the tradition of Embalmer.

She moaned softly, her lips parting prettily. He leaned forward waiting for that moment when their eyes met for the first time . . . well, again. She'd seen him at her house.

They fluttered open. She looked around the room frantically before zeroing in on him. Those almond eyes widened.

"How are you feeling?" he asked because he cared about her. He hadn't intended to double-dose her, but it had been necessary.

A scream ripped from deep down inside her soul followed by another and another.

"No, it's okay. You're okay. He won't hurt you."

But she wasn't looking at Mentor. She looked straight at him. He was the monster in her eyes. Perhaps Mentor had been right about her.

"Calm down."

"Shut her up," Mentor growled.

When she continued to scream, he clamped his hand over her mouth.

Was she unworthy after all? He'd been so certain about Veronica.

He could feel Mentor gloating. Everything he did wasn't up to Mentor's standards, and now he'd possibly screwed up again by insisting Veronica be part of their family.

With each beratement the truth became clear. He'd have to get rid of Mentor soon. Time for the mentee to shed his mentor's clutches.

Veronica stared up at him with terror in her eyes and tried to speak.

"I'm going to take my hand away. Don't scream or I'll have to put you under again. Do you understand?" She slowly nodded.

He lifted his hand. She didn't scream. "Do you know who I am?" She hurled the question at him.

"Of course. You're Veronica Turner."

"*Judge* Veronica Turner." She stressed the word judge. She'd gotten control over her emotions. Her fear now replaced with anger. "I know people in every branch of law enforcement as well as the government. Do you know what they'll do to you when they find you?"

His smile slipped a little. "That doesn't matter now. You're mine. I'm going to make you immortal." She continued to look at him as if he'd lost his mind, and he added, "You were chosen. You're worthy."

She fought against her restraints and cursed him. "I'll kill you—"

Her threat sent him over the edge. It reminded him of *her* and the way she'd treated him and the others.

He grabbed another syringe and injected it into her neck. Her wildeyed fear slowly faded. Her eyes closed. She was out.

"You've killed her. You overdosed her and killed her." Mentor's distain was clear. "I told you she wasn't worthy."

"Shut up!" He whipped toward the man he'd once adored and strode to within inches of his face. "Shut up, shut up, shut up. She's not your pick. She's mine, and she's perfect."

Mentor's expression never changed, but simply stared him down with cool disdain confirming him unworthy too. Perhaps one day Mentor would write that word above his mentee's dead body.

He went over to Veronica and felt for a pulse. Not a single heartbeat. "It doesn't matter. I can still make her part of the family."

"You ruined the process. She's bleeding from the puncture wound and from the mouth. It won't be the same. She's imperfect."

Mentor was right—he'd flawed her. Somehow, he held onto the rage burning inside and kept from grinding his words out. "It will be fine." He grabbed the hairbrush from the nearby table and began smoothing out her tussled strands while Mentor watched his every stroke.

I'm sorry. You are perfect to me. Still, he'd cheated himself of those precious moments with her before he'd taken her life. He'd let emotions get in the way.

Once Mentor was no longer in his head, he talked to her like he would if she were awake.

"I hope you enjoy your new home." He'd put a smile on her face. Her expression was far too stern. "You must hate having to deal with criminals all day long. Don't worry. You won't be stressed anymore." He remembered the deep purple dress he'd found in her closet and went over and picked it up. "Look. I chose this for you to wear. And those pretty brown boots. I'll take that creased brow away so that you can be happy when we talk."

He spared Mentor a look. "And you won't be alone. You'll have Tiffany for now. There will be others. More to come. We will have our own little family. Only it will be perfect." Not like the family he'd ended up with. A mother who neglected her children for drugs and a father he never knew.

But that was the past. His new family would be perfect. Filled with the most talented and beautiful people. The ones *he* chose to share his life with.

"First, I must get rid of your humanness." That's what he referred to the process Mentor had invented to drain the body of fluids and then replace it with a far more advanced embalming method, making his new family member immortal.

He finished brushing her hair and glanced lovingly down at her. In her handbag she had makeup and the perfect shade of lipstick to match the dress. She would be beautiful.

He attached the syringe that would remove her blood and sat down beside her, trying to snub Mentor.

"We can share each other's days. Oh, and you're right next to Tiffany. You'll like her."

He reached for her hand. Still warm and soft to the touch. Imagined her fingers entwined with his as they talked. Her smile. Shining eyes. He'd give her the most beautiful eyes. Perhaps with a hint of amber, he thought.

Once the blood was removed along with her organs, he did his best to close her up with the least amount of scarring to her perfect body.

"There. We're all done. That wasn't painful, was it?" He laughed at his own joke. Of course, it wasn't painful.

With her smile in place, he picked up the dress and carefully slipped it on her. After it was zipped up, he smoothed it into place.

"You look amazing." He stood back and admired her. "Your eyes practically sparkle."

"You are being foolish." Mentor's darkness intruded into this special moment. "There's no talking during this part."

"Maybe for you there isn't."

He retrieved Veronica's purse. "Now, for your makeup." He'd noted the brand she used. Very expensive. She deserved as much.

Once the base was applied, he added eye shadow and lipstick then stepped back to adore her. "Lovely. Simply lovely." He carefully lifted her into his arms. "Let me show you to your perfect resting place."

He carried her into the room where his immortals would all be placed. Tiffany smiled as he passed. He'd speak with her after he had Veronica settled in. He didn't want her to feel left out. "I have company for you, Tiffany. Meet Veronica."

Tiffany continued to smile, no doubt pleased to be so close to the lovely Veronica.

He stepped into Veronica's space, recreated to reflect her living room down to the same book he'd found on her coffee table during his many visits. Her favorite chair sat in the corner next to the side table, where a glass of wine had been poured for her. Veronica's reading glasses lay beside the wine. Next to that, a photo of himself with her and Tiffany and Mentor he'd photoshopped. A happy family that would soon be growing. He'd made one for Tiffany as well.

"Do you recognize this place?" He showed it to her. She was happy. He could tell from her smile she liked having her things close. "It's your living room, my sweet."

He carefully lowered her into the chair and arranged her hair and dress.

"There. You're all set." He glanced at the wine. "Your favorite Merlot. Enjoy."

With a final lingering look, he stepped out into the hall and stopped next to Tiffany, who waited patiently for his visit.

"How are you today, my dear?" He clasped her hand and looked into her eyes. "I hope you and Veronica will get to know each other better. I think you will be pleased with her."

He had no doubt they'd get along. And soon, he would have more family to share with them. So much more.

CHAPTER SIXTEEN

The key slipped into the lock. He was home. Soon, his heavy footsteps lumbered down the hall.

The scent of pure evil permeated every molecule of her being, and the familiar dread settled in around her. It took all her strength to leave the comfort of her safe haven—the tiny space in her bedroom closet where she found a small amount of peace—to face him again.

She'd prayed. All day long while he'd been working, she'd spent the time on her knees until they ached. Numbness seeped up her legs. She'd begged and pleaded with God to kill him and end her pain. God had other things in mind. Other plans. Or maybe He was simply not in the business of answering the prayers of sinners.

◆◆◆

Darkness pressed in all around. Hannah fought back a scream. She could feel the woman's fear as if it were her own.

"You okay?"

Hannah jerked toward Cooper's voice. He watched her with fresh worry. As the nightmare faded, her breathing returned to normal. Reality replaced the woman's fear. It wasn't real. *This* was real. They were still in the vehicle heading back to the hotel.

The lulling of the ride had rocked her to sleep. Since she'd been out of it, the weather had worsened into all out-blizzard conditions.

"Yes, yes, I'm fine." But she didn't sound it.

"Are you sure? You look like you've seen a ghost."

A haunt who lived in her dreams and who scratched and clawed for release into the real world. One day, she'd see him face-to-face and she'd have to kill him.

Hannah ignored Cooper's statement and leaned forward. "It's really coming down. How are you holding up? Do you need a break from driving?" Her voice still reflected the terror, and she struggled to disguise it from him.

She glanced over her shoulder to where Zeke busied himself on his laptop. He gave her a lopsided smile.

"I'm okay, but I'm ready to reach the hotel."

She noted the death grip Cooper had on the steering wheel.

"How close are we?"

"Several miles still." Zeke answered for Cooper.

As if to emphasize the danger facing them, the tires spun.

"I can barely see the road." Cooper leaned forward. The Suburban hit a patch of ice and did a 360-degree spin.

Hannah screamed and grabbed for the hand grip near the door.

"Hang on," Cooper yelled.

The SUV gained momentum within the spin. Whiteness flashed in a blur all around. A loud blast resounded through the deathly silent cab. One of the tires had blown, sending the vehicle careening toward the nearby woods. Each second chimed in time with Hannah's frantic pulse.

A moment later, the SUV plowed into the deep snow near the edge of the road, slowing its speed but not enough to keep the vehicle from slamming into a grove of fir trees. The momentum of the crash sent Hannah lurching forward, straining against the restraint of her seatbelt.

The crash was over in seconds. The shock took longer to subside.

"Is everyone okay?" Cooper looked from her to Zeke.

Both managed to confirm.

The Suburban had stalled out on impact. Cooper tried several times to revive it without any luck. "We'll need a wrecker to pull us out."

"There's no service." Zeke held his phone in several positions with the same results.

The vehicle's onboard emergency roadside assistance also failed to work.

"We're stuck until the storm lets up and we can walk out, or until someone comes along." Cooper blew out a frustrated sigh.

"And that could be hours in this type of weather." The temperature inside had already dropped considerably without the heating unit running.

"I heard an explosion," Zeke said.

"We must have hit something." Cooper told them it could have been anything. "Visibility was down to zero."

Hannah couldn't stop shivering. As much from the dream as the terrifying accident.

"There are some blankets in the back." Zeke must have seen her shaking. He reached over and handed Hannah and Cooper one before grabbing one for himself. "Since we have time, we might as well work the case. It will keep our minds off the storm and the cold."

Always the practical one. Hannah smiled at the clearly Zeke comment.

Hannah couldn't get something Isobel said out of her head. "I keep thinking about what Isobel said about Ellison asking her to deliver his notes to the man she calls his brother. She confirmed he wasn't one of Ellison's visitors, yet he must have kept in touch with the brother through the years."

"Before I lost service, I did my best to track the number Ellison gave her," Zeke told them. "It was a dead end."

"They could have been speaking for years. I had no idea," Cooper said in disbelief. "Of course, he'd know where the brother lived. Maybe he planned to have his brother carry on his killing or perhaps he was going to use him to reinforce his claims of being set up."

Hannah studied him curiously. "You think he was telling the truth?"

"No, I don't. I think he was trying to save himself by creating doubt. He killed those women like he killed my mother."

"Maybe he was working with this man he calls his brother," Zeke suggested.

Cooper's mouth thinned. "A family that kills together. . ." he stopped suddenly. "Did you hear that?"

Hannah listened. "Someone's coming. They'll never know we're here in this storm."

"I'll see if I can get their attention." Cooper opened the door against the wind and got out.

"We're coming with you." As soon as Hannah stepped from the vehicle, she landed mid-calf in deep snow.

Zeke grabbed her arm. "Careful."

She looped her arm through his and they joined Cooper. The three headed out to the road.

Headlights barely pierced the whiteout.

"The driver won't see us until he's right on top of us." Cooper returned to the vehicle and brought back one of the blood-red blankets.

The vehicle drew closer, its headlights becoming brighter. Cooper waved the blanket around. When the car didn't show any signs of stopping, he tossed it onto the passenger side of the windshield.

The car braked suddenly, spinning its tires. Thanks to the driver's slow speed, the results weren't as bad as theirs.

"Thank You, God," Cooper yelled before heading to the driver's side.

Hannah couldn't imagine how frightened the driver must be having been stopped so strangely.

Cooper leaned close and did his best to explain who they were. He pulled out his identification.

The driver slowly lowered the window slightly. "You guys scared me. I wasn't expecting anyone to be on the road." The man smiled and glanced at each of them.

There was something familiar about him that Hannah couldn't place. Impossible, surely. They'd never met. Just the remnants of the disturbing dream bleeding into this frightening moment.

"You guys need a ride somewhere?" An older man, he wore a watch cap pulled down over his ears. Brown eyes held nothing but a slight interest in them. Certainly, no sign he recognized Hannah.

Just her imagination.

"We'd appreciate it." Cooper told him they were staying on Grand Island at the Island Breeze. "I hope that's not too much trouble."

"Not at all. Hop in. Excuse the mess. I practically live in my car." He shoved fast-food wrappers from the passenger seat. "Name's Nolan Lewis." "Nice to meet you, Nolan. I'm Cooper. This is Hannah and Zeke."

"You all federal agents?"

Cooper chuckled. "We are. Thanks for the ride." Cooper turned to Hannah and Zeke. "Why don't you get in where it's warm? I'll grab our things and be right back."

"Sure thing." Instead of getting in beside Lewis, she climbed into the back seat while Zeke opened the passenger door next to Lewis.

"Just shove that stuff out of your way," Lewis told her. The back seat and floorboards were littered with trash.

Cooper returned with their computers and the sketchbook Isobel had given them. He slid in beside Hannah.

"Well, let's see if we can make it to the island without having an accident." Lewis appeared amused by his own joke. He put the car into Drive and eased down the road. "What are you all doing out here in the middle of nowhere?" Lewis stared at Hannah in the rearview mirror. "You were lucky I came along when I did. This road doesn't normally get much traffic."

"We're working a case," Zeke told him and shifted in his seat so that he could examine Lewis. "Do you live around here?" Zeke was a naturally curious person even when he wasn't investigating.

Lewis spared him a look before focusing on the road. "Nah. I'm a window salesman. I have a route all over the state. What's your case about?"

Cooper told him they really couldn't discuss the details of an active case.

"Wait, this isn't about that murder I heard about on Grand Island, is it?" He looked between the three waiting for confirmation.

"Again, we can't say." Cooper's tone held a touch of frustration in it.

"Oh, right. I get it." He winked at Cooper and changed the conversation to the weather. "I haven't seen a storm like this in years. You guys picked the wrong time to be investigating."

Hannah couldn't shake the feeling she'd seen Lewis somewhere before. For the rest of the trip, she tried to place it and couldn't.

When Lewis pulled into the parking lot for the Island Breeze, Hannah was grateful to get away from the strange man.

"You all take it easy out there," Lewis said, his attention once more on Hannah. "There are a lot of bad people around. You don't want to end up like one of your victims."

Hannah froze in place at the strange comment. The three watched Lewis drive away.

"What an odd thing to say," she whispered. "You don't think he's . . . ?"

"Our killer?" Cooper shook his head. "No. He's an odd bird. But he doesn't fit the description Isobel gave us."

Still, the name Nolan Lewis was imprinted on her brain. She wouldn't soon forget the strange encounter, and she wanted to check him out further.

"What happened to you?" Megan met them at the entrance. "I expected you back some time ago. I've been trying to reach you. With the storm coming in so unexpectedly, I've been worried."

Hannah explained the accident. "We'll need to have the vehicle towed."

"I'll call the rental company and let them know. They can send over a replacement. Come inside and warm up. The restaurant made a pot of chicken tortilla soup for us. It's delicious. There's cornbread as well."

The fire in the lobby beckoned. Hannah held her hands close. She was chilled to the bone and couldn't stop shaking.

Cooper stood beside her. She turned and found him watching her. His light-brown hair soaked from the snowfall. He had the profile of a hero. And she wanted more than anything not to have feelings for him.

A confused smile spread across his face. "Still thinking about Lewis?"

She slowly nodded. "I can't shake the feeling I've seen him before."

"He may just have that kind of face. I did a quick check on him. Appears clean."

Hannah tried to let go of her uneasy feeling. "Thank you. I'm sure it's just the case making me jumpy." She held his gaze and wished for so much more. The warmth from the fire melted the cold from her body. However, the winter storm in her heart would never end.

"Why don't we get something to eat?"

She was happy to follow him to the table where soup and cornbread warmed. Zeke had bypassed the food to dive into work.

She and Cooper carried their bowls over to where he sat talking to Megan.

Hannah pulled out her chair. "What's new on the missing judge?" She tasted the soup and closed her eyes briefly at its delicious flavor. "Her sister identified an outfit that was missing from her closet along with her purse. Her phone and house key were still at the house so . . ." "She didn't leave on her own accord," Hannah concluded.

"Exactly. Jack and the team are winding up their investigation there.

Her security cameras were remotely disengaged just like Giselle's and Tiffany's."

Cooper sat back in his seat. "We're looking at someone who knows how to disarm elite security systems. We need to find out if Giselle and Tiffany and Veronica had the same security firm handling their systems."

"Already did, and they were all different businesses," Megan told them.

"So, we're looking at someone highly skilled with the technology used to operate the systems. Enough to know how to disable them remotely." Hannah had no idea how they would find such a person.

"He won't be easy to locate simply by his ability to dismantle a security system. He could have taught himself how to do it. If so, that route will be a dead end." Cooper looked between them.

"You're right. Still, it doesn't hurt to check in with the home security firms around the state and see if any present or past employees send up a red flag. I'll search the criminal databases for any similar MOs." Megan jotted notes as she spoke. "Can we assume Giselle was found unworthy because of her drug and alcohol issues? Tiffany and Veronica don't appear to have any substance abuse problems as far as I can tell. They're both single—unlike Giselle." Megan shrugged. "I'm not sure if that's important or not."

"Probably not." Zeke's fingers clicked along the keyboard. "I remember reading about the victims from the original Embalmer case." He sat back in his seat. "Here it is. The women who were selected to be embalmed were both married and single. Same for the unworthy ones."

Hannah's hopes sank. "Let's focus on the unworthy victims from the past for a minute. Did any of them have a drinking problem or other issues that might condemn them as unworthy?"

"Not really," Zeke said. "All the women had careers. I couldn't find anything in the unworthy victims' pasts to warrant the condemnation."

"Whatever their sins are, they're known only to my father and maybe to this copycat. Can we get a side-by-side collage of all the women past and present?" Cooper asked.

Hannah frowned. "What are you thinking?"

He looked her way. "Maybe it isn't about who they are, but what they look like. Maybe he has a type."

CHAPTER SEVENTEEN

“Got it.”

Cooper and the rest of the team gathered around Zeke. The victims from the past and the three current ones did resemble each other slightly.

“They’re all professional women who have dark hair. It’s something,” Cooper said. Just not enough to move the case forward any in his mind.

“They all lived within about a hundred-mile radius of Rochester,” Hannah added. Which would put them within a short traveling distance. But why these women? “One thing I think we can agree on, at least for the women who were found worthy, it wasn’t a rage killing,” Hannah said. “They weren’t tortured. Quite the contrary. Their deaths came as peacefully as possible under the circumstances, unlike the ones that were condemned.”

Cooper hadn’t thought of it that way. “You’re right. It’s almost as if he treasured the worthy ones. They were intended to be his possessions forever.” Something Cooper had put off since they arrived couldn’t be left any longer. “When the weather clears, I’d like to take a ride over to my grandparents’ place.” The farm where Cooper had so many good memories growing up. But the memories had been destroyed along with his happy childhood by his father’s actions.

“You think the killer would use the same place as before?” Zeke asked, clearly doubtful.

Cooper shook his head. “Not really. I’m thinking the copycat might be using someplace nearby. He obviously idolized my father for whatever reason. If this is some long-lost brother I’m not aware of existing, then it stands to reason he'd want to recreate everything to match the original murders . . . and supposing he was rejected by the family, he'd be angered by that."

"Angry enough to frame your father?" Hannah pinned him with her gaze. She was referencing Oliver's claims of being set up.

"He wasn't framed, Hannah. I saw him murder my mother, remember? He killed all those women. He deserved his place in prison . . . and in hell."

He'd seen the same look of pity in her eyes before. He fought back feelings of frustration that must have shown because then Hannah asked about his grandparents.

"What were they like?"

If he didn't want to lose her as a friend, he'd have to get a grip on his emotions. "The nicest people you'd ever want to meet. Deborah and Ralph Ellison. They owned a hundred-acre apple farm outside of town. We went there every chance we got. We spent holidays there. I'd stay with them over the summer. They were good people who trusted God and loved their family."

"What happened to them?" Megan asked.

"Grandpa Ralph died of cancer. Grandma Deborah passed away a few weeks later. Her heart. I think she didn't want to go on without him. They'd been married close to sixty-five years."

"Sixty-five years?" Hannah's eyes widened. "They didn't have your father until later in their marriage?"

Cooper had never considered it before. "I guess. They were in their eighties when they passed."

"So, they'd have been in their early forties when Oliver was born. Back then, that would have been considered unusual."

"Yeah, I guess, although they never acted old. They were always doing something. Grandma taught Sunday school and played the piano at church. Grandpa still worked the farm—just the two of them." Hearing his past out loud, there were things he never questioned before that now didn't add up.

"Do you mind if I do a little checking into them?" Zeke asked quietly.

"You're thinking they might not be my grandparents?" Cooper couldn't fathom it.

"I'm not saying that." Zeke shrugged. "It just seems there may have been some things they kept from you."

"I don't mind. I hope you find some answers into the copycat's identity." Because right now they had very little beyond speculation.   Soon, the rest of the team returned from Veronica Turner's.

"Thank goodness, we made it. It's really nasty out there," Sierra exclaimed, shaking snow from her hair. "It took forever to get back here. Cell service is knocked out because of the storm."

"Did you find anything useful at the crime scene?" Cooper watched her remove her coat and hang it across the back of the chair.

Sierra looked his way. "Not really."

Jack poured coffee and wrapped his fingers around it as if for warmth. "There weren't any fingerprints left behind. We did find some blood droplets, however."

"You're kidding?" Finally, a lead that might yield the killer's ID.

"Our ERT team is hopeful. They're using the state police lab in Rochester to analyze the evidence. Bob's put a rush on the blood sample." It was something.

Cooper rose and stretched the kinks from his shoulders. He stepped into the lobby to clear his head and noticed the reservations clerk wasn't around. With the weather being the way it was, there wasn't much of a chance anyone would be reserving a room for a while.

Driving snow reduced visibility to just a few feet from the window. Darkness descended quickly even though it was barely four.

He saw her approach through the reflection in the glass. Hannah.

"How are you really, Cooper?"

He turned toward the real woman, leaving the ghost in the window reflection. "Honestly, I don't know. For my entire life the one thing I could always count on were my grandparents. I'm not sure how I'd feel if I find out they weren't who I thought."

She stood next to him and leaned her head against his shoulder. "You won't. They *were* who you thought."

He bit back a bitter laugh. "Like my father was who I thought he was? It doesn't work that way."

She lifted her head to him. "I wish I'd known what you went through."

He wanted to ask her if it would change her mind about them, but he already knew the answer.

"I guess we both have secrets that are hard to talk about."

She tensed and turned toward the window. "I guess we do."

She believed her life had a timestamp on it. She was living it as if waiting for death. How could he make her see no matter how much time she had he wanted to share it with her. If friendship was all she could offer, then he'd find a way to be happy with it.

He reached for her hand, surprising her.

Hannah faced him again.

"I know you're scared about dying, and I get it," he added when she would have pulled away. "You and I have a different take on death because we deal with it every day." He searched her face. "All I'm saying is I want to be part of your life. In whatever capacity that looks like."

She touched his cheek without answering.

"What is it?" There was something she didn't want to tell him.

She shook her head. "Nothing." She spotted something outside the window and stepped closer. "Did you see that?" "What?" All he saw was white.

"It's gone." She leaned in closer. "Cooper, I'm almost certain I saw Lewis's vehicle out there." She grabbed her coat and slipped her arms into it.

"Hannah, wait." Cooper snatched his coat and shrugged into it as he followed her out to the portico. He searched through the whiteout conditions. "I don't see anyone." Why would Lewis return to their hotel? Sure, he was odd enough, but he wasn't connected to their case . . . was he? "There's no one here. Let's go back inside."

After another moment of uncertainty, she went with him.

With her hands held out to the fire, he could see she was still troubled by the thought of Lewis being outside their hotel. She kept glancing out the window.

"He doesn't fit the description given by Isobel."

She sat down on the sofa. "I know. But don't you think it's strange that he was out there in the middle of the blizzard in the first place?"

Hannah was a seasoned agent and not one to go jumping at shadows. He recalled the small car that he'd seen behind them leaving the Witherspoon place. It, too, had been white. He hadn't noticed the make.

Cooper sat next to her and told her about the car.

"If it was Lewis, why would he be near our crime scene and then show up in the same area as Isobel's house?"

"I don't know." He grabbed his phone.

"Who are you calling?"

"The officers watching Isobel's place. I want to make sure she's safe." The officer in charge answered his call immediately. "Everything okay there?"

"All's quiet. Ms. Melendez is inside. We checked on her about ten minutes earlier."

Still, Lewis's strange behavior wouldn't let him go. "Keep your eyes open. And let me know if you spot anything unusual." Cooper ended the call and looked at Hannah. "She's safe." Yet why couldn't he believe it?

"Thank goodness. If the car you saw near the Witherspoon place was Lewis's, he'd have no reason to be there. He sells windows. I doubt the Witherspoons were having some installed, especially at this time of the year.

"You're right. It was odd that he'd be out in the middle of a blizzard." Cooper stood and waited for Hannah while wondering how many more loose ends would be thrown at them before some of them finally made sense.

CHAPTER EIGHTEEN

The silent condemnation was meant to portray Mentor's disappointment. In the past, knowing he'd disappointed his hero would have devastated him. Now, their time was coming to an end. He'd outgrown Mentor. His way of doing things was no longer necessary.

He scanned the images of his next victim while imagining how special their time together would be.

"Another beauty?" Mentor's voice dripped sarcasm. "Haven't you learned your lesson? Beauty fades. That quality I taught you to seek out lasts forever."

He rolled his eyes without looking at Mentor. "Yes, well, I see no reason why I can't have both. Tiffany was as beautiful as she was smart." Mentor snorted. "And what about her?" He meant Veronica.

"She had both as well. She was feisty."

"She's not worthy. You should have never selected her. I told you who the perfect one would be. I picked her out for you, and yet you had to do it your way, and look how it turned out."

He jerked toward Mentor. "How it turned out was perfect. I have Veronica and Tiffany. They are friends now."

Mentor smirked. "There will be issues. She will bring them to us, mark my words. She was too much for you. I tried to warn you. She caused you to bleed. If you bled at her house, they will find you, and it will be over.

I have selected our next worthy victim. The doctor."

He wasn't surprised by Mentor's choice. Mentor had a thing for her. He, on the other hand, had never trusted her. Mentor had deemed her the perfect victim. He'd wanted her before Giselle or Tiffany. Had never approved of Veronica. Now, after the debacle with Veronica, Mentor would insist.

Snapshots of the doctor lay scattered around the table. Mentor gazed upon them, no doubt remembering their romance fondly.

While he pretended interest, the doctor did not fit the image he had of his beauties. She'd gone off the deep end and disappeared off the grid. Of course, he'd been able to locate her, but, in his opinion, she wasn't worth the effort. She wasn't even part of the unworthy crowd.

The one he wanted would be flawless in every way. He hadn't known about her until he'd seen her at Giselle's home. Since then, he hadn't been able to take his mind off the lovely investigator. He'd been intrigued. She would make the perfect addition to their little family. She was one of them. Smart. Beautiful.

He laughed to himself, imagining Mentor's reaction when he showed up with *his* choice of victims and not the good doctor.

"What's so funny? Are you even taking this seriously?" He ignored Mentor's suspicions and pretended to study the photos of the doctor. He'd play along. Let Mentor believe his good doctor was the next victim. But she would never be. How could she? She was unworthy.

When Mentor seemed lost in the past, he pulled out his laptop, where he'd stored *her* images. So confident. Self-assured in her law enforcement skills. He touched her face on the screen. Perfect. Just perfect. His next beauty.

◆◆◆

Sometime in the middle of the night, the storm blew itself out. Nothing but blue skies waited outside. The snow had been cleared away from the portico. Though the day remained freezing, at least they wouldn't be traveling in a blizzard.

The rental company had brought over a new SUV after towing the injured one in for repairs.

For Cooper, the night had been endless. Sleep illusive. Too many spooks fighting for space in his head. What little he did manage was filled with images of Hannah. His father. His grandparents and the unknown man who might be his uncle.

Just before dawn, Cooper gave up and went downstairs as the kitchen staff were putting out breakfast pastries and coffee.

He'd downed his third cup and was going back for another when Hannah found him.

She stopped when she spotted his appearance. "How long have you been awake?"

He smiled wryly. "Don't ask."

She poured a cup of coffee and grabbed a muffin. "Couldn't sleep?"

"Not really."

Hannah seemed to realize he didn't want to talk about it. "Where is everyone?"

"We're the first." He pulled out a chair for her in the conference room they'd been using. "I'm going to give Jane a call and see if she's had any luck locating the supposed brother."

Hannah checked the time on her phone. "Oh, yeah, you're good. Jane is an early bird. By now, she's finished her morning workout and is deep into work."

Jane had been a natural fit. When she'd interviewed for the position, Cooper hadn't been so sure. She was outspoken and didn't hold back her opinion. After five minutes of conversation, he'd given his blessing. He liked her.

"Hey there, Coop. I didn't know you knew what this time of day looked like."

For some reason everyone at the BAU thought he was some type of party animal. Cooper didn't bother correcting them. At one time, they'd been right. He drank hard, partied harder, and went through women like water. But that was before he realized the destructive path he was on would lead to the same outcome as his father's. He didn't want to live like that any longer. And so, he'd talked to his adoptive father, who was a minister. He'd read Scripture with him. They'd talked about the God Cooper didn't have time for before. That talk had changed his life.

Now, he faked a laugh. "Just checking in to see if you've made progress on locating my dad's mysterious brother." The silence on the other end had him sitting up straighter. "You have."

"What's going on?" Hannah slipped into the chair beside him.

"I'm not sure." He put Jane on speaker. "Hannah's here with me."

"Hi, Hannah." Jane's less than enthusiastic reaction to Hannah proved the truth. Cooper wasn't going to like what she had to say.

"Just tell me," he said when the silence strained his shot nerves.

"I haven't been able to track down your father's brother yet, but I did find something interesting."

Cooper reached for Hannah's hand, instinctively needing her strength.

"I'm afraid there's no easy way to say this, Cooper. Your grandparents were not your real grandparents."

Cooper heard the words, yet they didn't make sense. "I don't understand. Of course, they're my grandparents." He remembered his conversation with Zeke the day before. Zeke wanted to dig deeper into them.

In Jane's typical straightforward way she said, "They aren't. They were your *great*-grandparents."

He was all set to deny it when little things didn't add up. The age difference between his grandparents and his father, for one.

"I'm sorry, but it's true. And you were right about your father living in Pennsylvania. He lived in a small town in Pennsylvania with his parents."

He became aware of Hannah squeezing his hand.

"Greg and Fern Ellison were Oliver's adoptive parents."

His world came crumbling around him. "Wait—what?"

"Oliver was adopted at age six by the Ellisons."

"Do you know what happened to his actual parents?" Cooper asked, his head spinning.

"There is no record of the birth parents. It could be because of a closed adoption, or because the child was abandoned. Maybe the birth parents no longer wanted any contact. Oliver could have been placed into foster care or ended up in an orphanage. Perhaps the birth parents gave him up because they couldn't take care of him. The possibilities are numerous, and in most cases unless the birth parents want to be involved in the child's life in some way, finding any record of them might be difficult."

"And if Oliver and his brother were separated because of the abandonment, we may never know his identity. What about the adoptive parents? Are they still around? The couple might remember the names of Oliver's birth parents. A last name to go by, if nothing else." Cooper's gut screamed there was something hidden in his past that was key to bringing the killer down.

Jane blew out a breath. "I'm sorry, Cooper, but they're dead. I found death certificates for Greg and Fern Ellison."

"How did they die, Jane?" Hannah asked.

"A home invasion gone bad. They were stabbed. Both were asleep in bed. The police report indicates the wife was killed first. Then the husband."

Hannah listened to the details of the attack before asking if anything was taken.

"Nothing of any value. Oliver was the one the police asked to go through the house and let them know what might be missing. A few TVs and other electronics. Some cash amounting to maybe a couple hundred dollars."

"So, nothing of much value."

Jane confirmed the police had wondered if the murders were staged to look like a home invasion. "The only person who would have benefited from their deaths was away at college. Oliver had a rock-solid alibi. He was with your mother."

Cooper remembered his parents telling him they'd met in college, but he had no idea about anything else.

"I can't believe he lied about my grandparents' deaths and pretended my great-grandparents were really his parents. His whole life was a lie, including who he was."

"Looks like it," Jane added quietly. "I'll keep digging. If there's another family member, I'll find them. Hopefully, they can shed some light."

Cooper thanked her and ended the call. "I can't believe it. Things just keep getting worse."

"He was hiding who he was even back then, though there's no evidence your father started killing until a few years before his capture."

He searched her face and then it clicked. "You think he killed them, and my mother provided an alibi for him?"

"It's possible. They were both stabbed. That was his MO for the unworthy victims. Maybe he found them unworthy and killed them."

"What's going on?" Sierra and Zeke came into the room followed by Jack and Megan.

Hannah squeezed Cooper's arm before telling them what Jane had found out.

"Unbelievable. It feels as if we're having to peel back layers and we're still no closer to getting answers." Jack sat at the table. "Who actually owns the property where your . . . great-grandparents lived?"

Cooper raised his hand. "That'd be me. The house is still standing. I went there a few years back," he said in answer to Hannah's obvious shock. "It's slowly wasting away. They deserved better, but every time I think about getting it fixed up, I remember those women my father bricked up inside the basement and I think that history needs to fade away."

"Are you sure you're up to going there today?" Hannah asked gently.

“We can handle it if not.”

“I want to go.” He had to finish this. However dark and ugly it ended up being, this was his story to finish.

CHAPTER NINETEEN

“Hannah before she left the hotel.

h, Miss London, this came for you.” The desk clerk stopped

Frowning, Hannah went over to the registration desk.
"For me?" Only her team and Bert knew she was here.

"Yes, ma'am." The young female clerk retrieved a folded piece of blue parchment paper with Hannah's name on it and handed it to her. "It was here when I started my shift."

Hannah unfolded the note and almost dropped the paper when she read those familiar words.

Beloved, now that I've found you again, I will never let you go. You will be with me soon. Now and always.

"Is anything wrong?" The young woman's smile faded.

"Who was on duty when the note was delivered?" The same wording as the note found on her kitchen table shattered her hopes that this might all be some juvenile prank. Someone had deliberately tracked her here to Grand Island. For what reason? Seeing it in the light of not being kids' pranks, the threat in those words scared the daylights out of Hannah.

"I'm sorry, there was no one on duty overnight. I have no idea who left the note."

"What about security coverage?" Hannah pressed. Most hotels had video surveillance around the lobby.

The young woman told her she'd tried searching through it. "It appears the storm took the system down for a while."

The storm or the person who left the note . . . just like the person they were chasing had dismantled the security systems belonging to his victims.

Her gut told her this wasn't the same person, but she couldn't be sure.

"Anything wrong?" Cooper asked when he got a good look at her worried expression.

Hannah stuffed the note into her shoulder bag. "No, nothing." She couldn't tell Cooper the truth. Not yet. She still wanted to believe there was some simple explanation that she could contain.

She thanked the clerk, who obviously thought it odd the way Hannah reacted. She'd probably seen a lot of strange things while working at the hotel.

Cooper searched her face. "Are you sure you're okay because—"

"I'm positive." She cut him off sharply, and immediately regretted it. "We should be on our way. There's a lot of property to search."

He slowly agreed. "Alright."

Zeke waited for them near the door. He tossed Hannah a look as if to say, "What's going on with you?"

Hannah ignored her brother's concerns and stepped from the hotel. The note had her rattled. She was being stalked. Soon, she wouldn't have a choice but to tell her team about the possible danger the person stalking her might pose.

Now that I've found you again . . . seemed to hint at a relationship that didn't exist. At least, not as far as Hannah remembered.

She searched around the all-but-empty parking lot and couldn't dispel the feeling of being watched.

Hannah thought about Lewis. The note at her house couldn't have been left by him. Lewis lived outside New York City. He sold windows for a firm there and travelled around the state. He'd worked the same job for two years. Before that he had a string of menial labor jobs until he seemed to have found his groove selling windows. Lewis didn't have so much as a parking ticket. Maybe he was just the type of person that gave off bad vibes.

Whatever was going on with Lewis, it wasn't connected to the person leaving her notes. They'd followed her somehow to the hotel where she was staying. That was alarming in itself. She'd have to let her team know about the potential danger soon. Before the stalker took his tactics to the next level.

"Want me to drive?" Zeke asked.

Cooper shook his head. "Naw. It will give me something to keep my mind off what's ahead."

Hannah slipped into the passenger seat and waited while he rounded the front of their new SUV. *Lord, he needs You.*

She'd struggled with her faith after losing Ellie. She didn't understand how God could take someone so good when there were so many bad people doing bad things to others. Embalmer and his copycat were a prime example along with the multitude of other cases waiting for them once they finished this one.

Cooper was hurting. She'd put her anger aside for him.

"Ready?" He looked her way.

Once more, Hannah was blindsided by this handsome man who meant so much to her. After more than nineteen years without a major hitch, she'd felt invincible. She'd thought perhaps she would be one of the transplant patients who lived a long life. Perhaps she could let love in.

And then Ellie died. Everything changed. She realized she was living on borrowed time.

"Hannah?" He shifted toward her. It was just the two of them, and the tension that had taken a hiatus returned.

"Yes, I'm ready," she murmured and focused ahead.

Seconds ticked by. She could almost imagine Zeke shaking his head.

Cooper started their replacement vehicle, a Nissan Armada, and left the shelter of the portico while Hannah struggled for calm. They had a case to solve. She had to focus on that.

"When was the last time you visited your great-grandparents before . . . ?" She didn't have to finish. Like her, Cooper's life was divided into before and after segments.

His hands tightened on the wheel then relaxed. She wondered if it was because of the tension between them or the memory from the past. "Maybe a couple of weeks before they died." He merged onto the highway that would take them off the island. "Looking back, I see there was stress between my parents. I'd catch them bickering. When I'd come into the room, they'd pretend everything was fine. I think my mother suspected my father was cheating on her." He laughed, a bitter sound that resounded through the vehicle. "I guess he was, only not the way mom thought."

She couldn't imagine how difficult that day must have been for him. "Did your great-grandparents ever mention anything about Pennsylvania?"

"Never. They treated my father like he was theirs. I never thought anything about the age difference. They were all about us having fun when we were there . . ." He stopped suddenly, and she looked at his profile. He'd remembered something.

"What is it?"

"There was something strange that happened once. My father and great-grandfather were in the barn talking. They didn't know I was there. I heard them arguing about someone. Grandpa said, 'He's got to go. He's causing problems.' They were looking at the gelding Grandpa kept. I just assumed he meant the horse was acting up and he'd have to trade him."

"Maybe he was speaking of someone," Zeke interjected. "Like the person in your father's drawing."

Cooper shot him a look through the rearview mirror. "It's possible. My father and great-grandfather never seemed to have a disagreement before, but they were arguing about something or someone that day."

Hannah's cell phone rang. "It's Isobel." She answered, putting it on speaker. "Is everything okay?"

"I'm not sure. I tried to reach my police protection team, but they're not responding. I can see them sitting in their patrol car—all of them in one vehicle. They're not moving, Hannah."

"Lock the doors and keep your shotgun close."

Isobel didn't respond.

"Isobel! Isobel, did you hear me?"

A scream reverberated through the phone.

"He's got her."

Zeke tried to call the officer in charge. "He's not answering. I'm calling backup to the location."

"We have to go there now," Hannah said, her voice shaken.

Cooper didn't hesitate. He whipped the Armada around and headed for the interstate, flooring the gas pedal.

"We're on our way to you now. Stay inside and keep the doors—" The call with Isobel ended abruptly. Hannah tried it again. Straight to voicemail.

"Jack and the team are meeting us there along with local police." Zeke had been on a call with the team.

"This is bad. This is *so* bad." Hannah kept trying Isobel's phone, praying it had all been a mistake. Yet with every unanswered try, her fear grew. Isobel was no longer able to answer her phone.

It felt like forever before they reached Isobel's house. By the time they arrived, the local police were there already canvassing the scene.

Cooper shoved the SUV into Park. Hannah identified herself and her team to the chief. "Are they alive?" The police cruiser was swarmed by law enforcement.

Chief Killian's grim expression was all the answer she needed. "I'm afraid not. They were all stabbed. I'm guessing Douglas and York were killed first. Then Harper and Tennison." He blew out a breath. "This is a terrible thing. They were good men. I'll need to notify their families soon."

"What about the woman inside the house?" Hannah's heart sank when the chief confirmed Isobel was missing.

"There had to be more than one person involved to take out my officers without them getting a chance to fight back. I've called in the state police. They're shutting down all roads leading into the area. Hopefully, we can catch the perps before they leave the county." Chief Killian looked over his shoulder as the medical examiner arrived.

"I'm so sorry for your loss, Chief," Cooper told the lawman. "Do you mind if we take a look inside the house?"

"Go ahead. Crime scene is in there now." The chief started toward the medical examiner.

Before they went inside the house, the rest of their team arrived.

Zeke brought them up to speed. "Chief Killian seems to believe the killer is acting with someone else. What do you think, Cooper?"

Cooper struggled visibly with his emotions. He swallowed several times before responding. "There was no proof my father ever worked with anyone. He was the only person responsible for the murders, despite his claim of being framed.”

Hannah agreed with Cooper. She was certain the killer would want to act alone to claim all the glory for himself. “It doesn’t make sense that the copycat who has followed your father’s MO almost religiously would suddenly bring someone else in on the murders.”

“If not, then he is cunning enough to take four trained officers down.” Jack looked up at the house. “Let’s see if anything jumps out inside the house.”

After they’d slipped booties over their shoes and put on gloves, they went inside, where the county’s crime scene unit was busy collecting evidence.

“I’m going to speak to the tech in charge.” Jack stepped away. The ERT unit would be taking over, but they could use the locals’ assistance.

Hannah looked around at signs of a struggle. “She fought him. Perhaps we’ll get lucky on DNA.” The blood droplets left at Veronica’s house had been determined to belong to an unknown male.

Jack joined them once more. “Bob’s people are on their way. In the meantime, let’s stay out of the way as much as possible but fan out. See if you can find anything useful in locating the doctor.”

“We’ve got the living room.” Sierra looked to Zeke, who agreed.

“There’s a barn at the back. Cooper, why don’t you and I see if there’s anything back there?” Hannah stepped outside, still reeling from the brazenness of the killer.

She and Cooper headed toward the barn, where they’d first met Isobel.

“I sure hope the state police were able to get roadblocks set up in time.” Hannah tried to hold onto hope, and yet there were literally dozens of small roads around the county. They couldn’t barricade them all.

Inside the barn, nothing appeared out of place.

Cooper looked around. “He didn’t come in here.”

Something caught Hannah’s attention. A box sitting on the floor had been opened. She went over and peered inside. “It’s a journal.” She looked over her shoulder at Cooper. “I think she left it this way on purpose. Isobel wanted us to find this.”

Hannah opened the journal. Words jumped off the page.

He's alive.

"Who do you think she's talking about?" She flipped the page.

"My father," Cooper murmured, his tone flat. "My father's alive."

Hannah jerked his way. "That's not possible. He was stabbed in prison. There's a death certificate." As she continued to read the journal it soon became clear Cooper was right.

"He faked his death. Oliver's injuries were serious, but not fatal. Isobel declared him dead and signed his death certificate partly because she thought herself in love with Oliver but mostly because she was afraid of him. She gave him a drug to slow his breathing tremendously." She scanned the page. "The effects of the drug only lasted a short time. Oliver's brother took possession of him. She never saw Oliver again." Hannah closed the journal. "He didn't die in prison.'"

"We've got to tell the others." Cooper headed for the door. "We've got to get to him before he kills Isobel." Hannah followed him outdoors.

Cooper told Jack what they'd discovered. "He's alive. Isobel helped him fake his death."

Shocked, Jack took the journal from Hannah and read the confession. "Unbelievable. This changes everything. We need to let the state police know they're looking for a convicted killer as well as his accomplice, which is possibly Ellison's brother. How would he get her out of the area without using any of the main roads?"

Cooper shook his head. "He obviously wouldn't use the way we came in." He tried to bring up Google Maps, but the service was sketchy.

Hannah found the chief and updated him on what they believed. "Are there alternate routes less traveled to get out of the county?"

He pointed toward the road. "This leads out of the county, but there's some rough terrain ahead. You wouldn't get there by using a car without four-wheel drive capability." Hannah thanked him.

"What are you thinking?" Jack asked once they were out of earshot of the chief.

"I think it's worth a try. We're wasting our time here. Jack, I'd like permission for Cooper, Zeke, and myself to try and cut off Ellison before he gets away."

"Go." Jack didn't hesitate.

Zeke overheard his name and came over. "What's going on?"

"We'll explain on the road." Cooper shed his booties and gloves and got behind the wheel.

Zeke climbed in behind him.

Once Hannah was in the passenger seat Cooper fired up the Armada.

Hannah couldn't imagine how frightened Isobel must be seeing Ellison again. She was clearly terrified of him.

Cooper turned the vehicle around and headed for the road while Hannah explained what they'd found in the journal.

"Wait—you're saying Ellison, the original Embalmer, is still alive?" Zeke was just as stunned as they were. "How is that possible?"

"Isobel was the doctor who treated him. She declared him dead. The warden and the rest of the team would have trusted her."

"Why would she do it?"

Hannah had wondered the same as Zeke. "I think she was too frightened to stand up to him."

"I can't believe that monster is still alive." Cooper appeared in a state of shock.

Hannah touched his arm.

It didn't take them long before Hannah saw why the chief had warned about the road.

Deep snow still littered the road where little sun penetrated.

"Tire tracks." Cooper pointed ahead. A single set of imprints confirmed they were on the right track.

"I'm calling it in." Zeke grabbed his phone.

"Looks like he's using tire chains." Hannah leaned forward to get a better look.

"You're right. They came prepared, and they have a head start on us." Cooper met her gaze. Hannah knew what that meant. If they lost the vehicle, Isobel would die.

There were spots that made it impossible to go more than a few miles an hour.

"State police are on the way to head Ellison off." Zeke read the text from his phone. "I don't like this one little bit."

Hannah felt the same way. If Ellison and his accomplice had taken Isobel, they'd probably been watching her for a while. They'd know the route to take to get away from her house quickly.

Cooper braked suddenly, drawing Hannah's attention to him.

"Why are you stopping?"

He pointed to the road ahead. A tree had gone down in front of them.

All three got out and examined the damage.

"It's been cut," Zeke pointed to clear evidence a chainsaw had been used to down the tree.

The Embalmer had known they'd come after him and had effectively taken them out of the chase.

CHAPTER TWENTY

 worth it. Her attention flew past him to where Mentor

ou!" Doctor Melendez's fear almost made the compromise
watched. Revulsion replaced her fear.

Her reaction was everything he'd hoped for. "That's more like it. Did you really think you could run away from us?" He turned to Mentor and pictured wiping that pleased expression off his face. "You aren't worthy." He brought out the knife.

"What are you doing?" Mentor demanded. "She is worthy. She's my choice."

"But not mine. You betrayed us. *Me.* You were never worthy." Before Mentor could react, he repeatedly slashed the good doctor's throat, taking out his anger at her and Mentor with each cut.

"How dare you!" Mentor seethed. "You had no right. She is worthy. I-I loved her."

He whirled toward the man he'd once admired, the knife raised. "You love no one. Not me. Not your family. Certainly not her. Now, leave me alone."

This will be the perfect gift for the son Mentor so idolized. Mentor had showed a love toward his son that he hadn't for his own brother.

He dipped his gloved finger into the blood pooling on the dusty floor and wrote the sentence she deserved. Unworthy. She'd tried to break them apart. Mentor would have been happy to live with her after leaving that prison if *he* hadn't stepped in.

"Time to go. They'll come here eventually. We need to get back to your place. It's time to find the next beauty."

Mentor stared at the woman dying on the floor as if he couldn't fathom what had happened.

"Go." He barked the order and then smiled at Mentor's frightened reaction. It pretty much sealed *his* place in command.

The vehicle waited. He climbed behind the wheel and drove the distance to their special entrance that no one would ever suspect.

From here on out, Mentor's wants would take the back seat to his. He was now fully in control. Mentor would have no say in choosing his next beauty.

He already had her in his crosshairs and couldn't wait to make her part of their family.

CHAPTER TWENTY-ONE

"T while studying the massive tree. "We might as well turn around."

here's no way we can move it on our own," Cooper said

"State police are at the spot where this road meets a county one. There's no sign of a vehicle being down that way."

Cooper couldn't believe it. "The vehicle must have left the road somewhere after he took the tree down and before it joined the second road."

"He could still be around somewhere. We need air support." Hannah called Jack and told him what the state police had said.

"I'll get choppers in the air right away," Jack told her. "The perps obviously knew the layout of the land well enough to have an alternate route carved out."

"We're coming your way." Hannah ended the call while Cooper struggled to get the SUV turned around on the tiny road.

They returned to Isobel's property and stopped near the house. ERT had arrived.

Jack and Sierra stood on the porch talking to the police chief.

"Choppers are airborne," Jack told them.

Cooper had a bad feeling their efforts would be in vain.

Soon ERT and the county's crime scene techs began carrying evidence bags from the house.

"Anything useful?" Cooper asked Bob, who stopped to give them an update.

"Not sure. We found blood. We'll see if it belongs to our victim or the perp."

Jack's phone rang. He stepped away to take the call.

"That'll be the air backup," Cooper whispered to Hannah. "They struck out."

Jack finished the call and confirmed Cooper's assumptions. "They'll widen their search. State police are canvassing roads around the area and have set up roadblocks."

Cooper could see Jack didn't believe they'd catch the killers either. "They're probably out of sight by now."

"No doubt. We can't do anything here," Hannah said watching the activity going on around them. "We should go to your property and have a look. Maybe something there will help us figure out the identity of your father's brother."

"Go." Jack gave his permission. "If you find anything—"

Cooper turned around as he headed for the Armada. "You'll be our first call." He felt numb inside as they left the crime scene. His father was still alive. The idea of Oliver Ellison keeping track of him all these years turned his stomach.

"Is there anything else that might be useful in the journal?" There had to be more. They were missing something. Cooper didn't believe for a minute that his father hadn't been keeping tabs on Isobel.

Hannah picked up the journal. "The next entry is four years after her admission to helping Ellison escape. 'Someone has been on my property. I found a set of footprints in the snow from while I was away getting supplies in town. They were all around my house. He wanted me to see them. I know it's Oliver. He's watching me. I've felt it before. He's going to kill me.'"

Cooper's brain dissected the entry. "But he didn't. That was more than six years ago. Did she see any other evidence of him around the place?"

Hannah turned the page. "This entry is two weeks later. 'Maybe I'm wrong. There's been nothing since I came home and found the tracks in the snow. It could have been a hunter who got lost.'"

"Or he decided to keep his surveillance a secret from her." Cooper had no doubt his father would continue to watch her through the years. "I wonder why she didn't leave when she spotted the tracks. She was obviously living in fear."

"Maybe she couldn't afford to." Zeke pointed out how meager the doctor lived. "She hasn't worked a job since she left the prison. She could be running low of funds."

"Possibly." Still Cooper wondered if she were as frightened as she clearly was why not sell the place to free up funds so she could leave. He didn't believe Isobel would ever report Oliver because by doing so, she'd incriminate herself in his escape.

He reached the turnoff to the road that would take him to his greatgrandparents' farm. The blanket of snow surrounding the countryside brought back fond memories. Each year, his family would cut down their Christmas tree from the woods near the farm.

Cooper struggled to reconcile those memories with the lies he'd been told by his father and his great-grandparents.

The beginning of the property came into view. The fence around the place was in disrepair. The last time he'd been here he'd seen the damage left behind by too many winters on an empty home.

"This is the start of the farm," he told his teammates.

"It's beautiful." Hannah's attention went to the passing scenery.

"It is." He'd always loved this place. His grandparents loved him, and they obviously had their reasons for keeping secrets. He'd never wanted to look through the house for evidence before. The police and FBI had searched it after finding the embalmed women. By then, he'd been long gone living with his new family. He'd never heard anything about evidence uncovered.

"Did they find anything at the house?" Cooper asked Hannah because he knew she'd read the case files.

"Not really. Nothing to give answers into why your father became the Embalmer. And I didn't read anything that indicated the couple who once lived here were not your grandparents. That secret was buried deep."

He slowed as the driveway appeared up ahead. Cooper pulled in and stopped. He'd been so certain he could handle it. Now he wasn't so sure.

"You okay, Coop?" Zeke leaned forward and clasped his shoulder. The worry on his friend's face was clear in the mirror.

"Yeah, I just need a minute." Cooper got out and moved to the front of the vehicle then leaned against it.

Hannah looped her arm through his and waited with him.

Cooper nodded. "It's like my entire childhood is nothing but a lie."

She leaned her head against his.

"Um, guys." Zeke knelt in front of them.

"You're going to get through this," Hannah murmured. "You have me. Zeke. The team."

He so wanted to believe her, but from where he was right now, he couldn't see normal much less find his way back to it.

"Guys." It was Zeke's tone that grabbed Cooper's attention.

He focused on his friend. "What?"

"Someone's been here. Recently." Zeke pointed to tire tracks in the snow. "Looks like more than one set of tracks."

"I'm calling it in." Hannah pulled the phone from her pocket. "We need backup." She explained what happened and listened for confirmation before signing off. "They're on their way now. Jack's radioing for Rochester PD to back us up. How far is it to the house?"

Cooper realized what she meant. They'd have to walk in to have the element of surprise. "Quarter of a mile." Cooper unholstered his weapon. "We stick to the trees at the edge of the road in case they have someone on lookout."

Hannah and Zeke confirmed, and they started for the side of the road.

Would he find his father here? No matter how hard he tried, Cooper couldn't wrap his mind around facing the ghost from his past that he'd hoped would remain buried along with all the unimaginable things his father had done in the name of evil.

CHAPTER TWENTY-TWO

As they approached the house, Hannah studied the surroundings. "There's no sign of a vehicle." From their viewpoint, she could see the side, back, and front of the house. A barn sat a little way off to the right near the front.

Cooper told her that was where the farming equipment was kept. "They could have parked on the opposite side."

"Let me check it out." Zeke started for the back of the house.

Hannah stopped him. "We'll go together." The last thing they needed was an ambush.

Zeke led the way.

"I don't like this. What reason would anyone have to be here unless it's my father and his partner?"

She couldn't answer that question. At the back of the place, they had a clear view of the side. No vehicle there either.

"He could have hidden it in the barn." Hannah's thoughts swirled with possibilities. "It makes sense that your father would come back here." Had he brought Isobel here to join the rest of his victims?

"There's a door at the back." Cooper indicated the place where the backside of the barn met encroaching woods.

They edged toward the entrance. The door appeared stuck from years of sitting unattended. Cooper yanked it from its frozen grip and went inside. "The power's been off for years." He used his flashlight app to search the large open space littered with decaying equipment.

"There's no one here." Zeke stepped from the building. "Whoever came here left soon after. The two sets of tracks must be from the vehicle coming and leaving the property."

It made sense.

"Let's check the house." Cooper headed along the side of the barn and crossed the yard. He stopped near the house and pointed. "Footprints." Two sets in the snow.

With his weapon at the ready, Cooper stepped up on the porch.

Right away, Hannah noticed something was off. The door had been left open . . . as if a sign for them to know someone had been inside.

Hannah gripped the Glock tight as she and Zeke followed him into the house.

The footprints led to what had once been the kitchen.

"The basement," Cooper said in a flat voice. "He wants us to go to the basement." He reached for the door handle. It turned freely in his hand.

Hannah used her flashlight app to illuminate the stairs as they followed the wet footprints.

Once they reached the bottom of the dusty basement, the fading prints turned left toward a crumbling brick wall.

"That's where my father kept his beauties, as he called them." Cooper led them toward the place where the wall had been compromised.

The moment Hannah's light shined in the space where Oliver Ellison had kept his special trophies, she gasped.

A woman's body lay crumpled on the floor.

"Oh, no." As Hannah neared, she realized who it was. "Isobel." She felt for a pulse. "She's still alive. Call an ambulance."

Isobel's throat had been slashed. There were multiple cuts all over her body. Above where she lay, a single word had been written in blood.

Unworthy.

Hannah unwrapped her scarf and used it to stem the flow of blood pouring from Isobel's throat while fighting back tears. She'd convinced the woman to trust her. Told her they'd protect her, and yet nothing was further from the truth. Because Isobel trusted them and they'd gotten her involved when she clearly didn't want to be, she was in critical condition.

"Ambo's on its way," Zeke confirmed. He knelt beside his sister. "This isn't your fault."

"Isn't it? I talked her into cooperating." She held Isobel's hand in her gloved one. If she were going to die here, Hannah wanted to make sure she knew she wasn't alone.

Vehicles moved in. "That's our people." Zeke rose and went out to meet them.

Cooper dropped down beside her. She glanced over at him and realized he was praying. She reached for his hand with her free one and joined him.

Isobel needed God's healing to get through this.

A siren wailed down the county road. Soon its sound grew louder as it neared the house.

EMTs and their team rushed inside the basement.

"Let's give them room to work." Cooper helped Hannah up.

She and Cooper joined the rest of the team silently watching as the EMTs did everything that could be done to save Isobel.

They worked quickly to get Isobel ready to transport.

Hannah and Cooper followed them out to the ambulance. The paramedic in charge told them which hospital they'd be transporting her to. With lights and sirens, the ambulance left the property at a rapid pace.

"I can't believe this happened." Hannah ran her hand through her hair and realized her glove was covered in blood.

"He's mocking us—no, he's mocking me. Tying everything back to his original crimes." A wintery look entered Cooper's eyes.

"We'll catch him. We have to catch him," Hannah stressed. Yet for years no one had been looking for Oliver Ellison because they'd believed he was dead.

Jack and the rest of the team emerged from the house. "ERT's on their way here now." Jack looked around the property. "Did he just come here to kill the doctor as a taunt?"

Cooper ran his hand over his eyes. "I have no idea. Obviously, the man I thought I knew never existed."

Hannah's heart went out to him. The blows just kept coming. "We'll leave the house for ERT to investigate. Let's spread out across the property and see if he left anything else behind."

She stuck close to Cooper. They started past the barn and walked toward the apple orchard.

"There are no footprints this way." She pointed to the ground. "But they could have come here before the snow covered their tracks. Maybe we'll find something useful."

Cooper didn't appear to be listening. He was lost in his own dark thoughts. She continued to search the countryside. There were dozens of apple trees on the old farm.

"How far does the orchard go?"

Cooper roused himself from his thoughts. "We're about halfway through them."

She was amazed by the enormity of the farm.

Her cell phone received an incoming text. "It's Jack. He's calling us back to the house. ERT's here. He wants us to return to Grand Island to go over everything. Looking around out here is a waste of time anyway."

Cooper stared at the massive number of trees. "You're right. There's nothing here."

The Armada had been moved to allow for Jack's team and the ambulance to enter the property.

She slipped into her seat and lay her head against the headrest as Cooper followed Jack and Sierra from the property.

Hannah said a silent prayer. "I sure hope Isobel makes it."

"Me too." Cooper's grip on the steering wheel was deathlike.

"Here's something interesting," Zeke said and read a message from Chief Killian. "Looks like there's an old four-wheeling trail right after where that tree was cut down. He must have taken it. According to the chief, there are miles of them all around the area. How would he have known that?"

Hannah thought about the question. "He had to have been planning to take Isobel for a while. Why would he judge her as unworthy? Because she talked to us?"

Cooper nodded. "He'd see it as an act of betrayal." Cooper's frown deepened. "My question is . . . why wait until now to start killing again? It's been years since he escaped."

Hannah had wondered the same. "There have been no records of any murders like Embalmer's since his capture. I had Jane confirm," she told him when Cooper raised his brow. "Maybe something set him off recently. Perhaps he was happy living a life of obscurity until something triggered the urge to kill again."

"Like maybe the return of this person he claims is his brother? On that subject, Jane sent me something she found." Zeke handed her the laptop he'd been working on.

"What am I looking at?" Hannah asked.

"A newspaper article from Pottsville, Pennsylvania about the same home invasion where Oliver's parents died. Remember Jane mentioned Oliver's parents had died in one. This is a later report claiming the home invasion appeared to be staged. I believe Jane mentioned as much. It was believed the father killed the mother then himself."

Hannah scanned the article. "The timing's right. But why did the police claim a home invasion in the beginning?"

"Not sure." Zeke pointed to the place in the article. "Looks like the original investigators were removed from the case and new detectives assigned."

"The removed detectives must have rushed to solve the case and missed something," Cooper said.

"Wait, this is interesting." Hannah reread the article to make sure it was correct. "The reporter spoke to Oliver, who claimed his father was under a tremendous amount of pressure at his work . . ." She stopped reading, her attention stuck on Greg Ellison's profession. "Greg owned a mortuary."

"That can't be a coincidence," Zeke said. "Maybe that's where the fascination with embalming came from."

"It would stand to reason Oliver would have at least visited the mortuary from time to time." Hannah continued reading. "Anyway, Oliver claimed the business was suffering financially and his father began drinking heavily. He believed Greg may have snapped and killed Fern, his wife. Then realized what he'd done and took his own life."

"Was there an insurance policy on the couple?" Cooper asked.

Hannah checked. "Nothing listed. We'll have to dig deeper." She handed the laptop back to her brother.

"I'll see if I can access the police records from back then." Zeke's fingers clicked the keys on the computer.

"Obviously, there's more to the story than what the police believed."

Hannah searched Cooper's face. "You think your father might have killed them both and staged the scene? The cause of death does fit his profile."

"I wonder if he lied about having a brother as well. Maybe he found a groupie he treated like a brother." She remembered something that had been part of the Embalmer's victims found at the Ellison farm. She retrieved her tablet and brought up the file on those victims. "All of your father's embalmed victims were found with names written near them. My sister Callie. My little sister Tonya. They each were displayed in a space that was later confirmed to match a room at their house. They'd become family to him. I wonder if he had sisters who weren't adopted with him. He was trying to recreate his family."

"But he had a family. Myself. My mother. Why would he need sisters and . . . and why weren't there any male victims?" His gaze bored into hers. "Because his brother is still alive. The initials P.A. Did he have sisters in the past who died?"

"It's possible. We need to find out. If something happened to his sisters, maybe that's why he's tried to replace them with women he embalms."

The thought was horrifying, and yet in a twisted way it made sense. But with no record of any other children at the Ellison household, what family was Oliver really trying to replace?

CHAPTER TWENTYTHREE

Cooper didn't understand anything anymore. Everything he'd once believed true about Oliver Ellison had crumbled around him. His dad had lied about so much. Cooper was certain this was just the tip of the iceberg of what would be uncovered.

"There's news on Isobel." Hannah read a text. "She's in critical condition. She lost a lot of blood and hasn't regained consciousness."

"But she's alive. That's good news." Cooper pulled under the portico of the hotel beside the SUV driven by Jack.

Megan met them at the entrance. Cooper could tell she had something important.

"A call came in to the Grand Island police. Detective Siegler took the call from a woman claiming she knows who killed Giselle Witherspoon and took the other women."

Nothing prepared Cooper for this. "You're kidding? We need to speak to her."

Megan shook her head. "That's just it. She'll only talk to you, Cooper. She said she's scared of the person responsible and wants to meet somewhere safe."

"She asked for me by name?"

"She asked for Cooper Ellison."

The name he'd once been so proud of slapped him in the face. "Did she give a name?"

"She did not. She did, however, leave a number." Megan gave it to him. "And before you ask, it's a burner phone."

"You should call her right away, Cooper," Hannah told him. "Put her on speaker and let us listen in. You can't out rule the possibility this is just some kook who's fascinated with the case. Under no circumstances should you meet her alone. She could be setting you up."

"For what? You think my father wants to kill me?" It didn't make sense to Cooper. His father had never once tried to reach out through the years.

Hannah touched his arm. "I'm saying you have to be careful."

"She's right." Jack agreed. "You're not meeting her alone. Get her on the phone, and let's see what she has to say."

With the team gathered around the conference table, Cooper punched in the number for their mystery witness. The call went to voicemail. Cooper glanced around at his people before redialing. This time a woman answered.

"Hello? Who is this?" She sounded terrified.

"Cooper Ellison. You wanted to speak with me."

His heartbeat ticked off the seconds until she responded. "In person. It's not safe over the phone."

"This is a secure line, and you're using a burner. It's safe." "How did you know this was a burner phone?" Her tone accused. "Did that female cop bug my phone?"

"That's not how it works. You're safe, I promise. What do I call you?"

"I'm not giving you my real name. You can call me Worthy."

The fake name sent chills down Cooper's spine. Certainly not a coincidence she'd chosen it.

"You told Detective Siegler you know who killed Giselle Witherspoon. How would you know that unless you were there?"

Worthy huffed out an angry sigh. "I told her I know who killed the dancer and took the others. I didn't tell her I was there because I wasn't. If you're just going to try and frame me for something I wasn't involved in, then we have nothing to talk about."

Cooper forced himself to slow down the questions. Worthy was spooked enough as it was. "I'm not accusing you of being involved. I just want to hear how you know all of this."

Seconds ticked by. "Because he told me."

"He? Who are you talking about?"

More hesitation had Cooper's frustration growing.

"My brother."

Brother. He couldn't determine her age, but it couldn't be his father she spoke of because there wasn't a record of any sisters. "Your brother is the killer?"

"Yes. He kept in touch with me through the years. And the others."

"You have more sisters?" Cooper recalled what Hannah said about the women his father embalmed. They were his sisters. His family. "What's your brother's name?"

Worthy remained silent for so long Cooper believed she'd hung up. "Are you still there?"

Her breathing could be heard. "I am. Look, he's the only family I have. I was passed through several foster families before I ended up at the orphanage with my brother. No one wanted us. When I aged out, I was lost and alone. He was always there for me."

She had loyalty to her brother, but she knew about his crimes and was torn.

"I know you care about him, but he's a killer, Worthy. He'll keep on killing until he's caught. Help us catch him before he can hurt anyone else. Or you."

"He'd never hurt me."

"What about the other women he's taken? He'll kill them." When she didn't answer, he wondered if the killer already had. "There were others. He killed several other women more than twenty years ago."

"That's not true. H-he wasn't even in the country at that time."

Cooper looked around at his people. If Worthy were telling the truth and the person she believed killed those women wasn't in the US, then she wasn't talking about his father. "You know my name. Who my father is and what he did. Giselle Witherspoon was killed using the same MO as my father. By your brother."

"This was a mistake." The call ended.

Cooper slammed the phone against the table, his frustration getting the better of him. He tried reaching Worthy several more times with the same results. "She's not answering."

"Give her time to process what you said." Megan patted his shoulder.

"Megan's right," Jack said. "She reached out before. It's possible she'll call again. She has your number. For now, let's go over everything we know so far. Hannah, is there anything else in the journal?”

“I’m not sure. With everything else that happened, I didn’t read through it all. Let’s see.” She flipped through to the last page she’d viewed. “Wait . . . I can’t believe this.”

Cooper sat up straighter in anticipation.

“Isobel goes into greater detail about what she and Ellison spoke about before his escape. He told her his brother killed their father later on.” She looked to Cooper. “Isobel regretted not going to the police after Ellison faked his death. She loved him but I think she was more frightened of him.”

Cooper frowned. “That’s not possible. The Ellisons never adopted anyone else.”

“Maybe he was angry and killed Oliver’s adopted parents for revenge because they took Oliver and not him?”

“I guess it’s possible.” Hannah’s theory was possible. Still, Cooper wasn’t convinced. He drummed his fingers on the face of the phone. “Worthy claimed her brother killed Giselle and took Tiffany and Veronica. I wonder if she knew about Isobel?”

“Probably. He obviously confides in her.” Sierra went to refill her coffee.

“Let’s suppose for a second that what Worthy said is true and the brother Isobel spoke of is the same as Worthy’s brother.”

“Something must have happened to Oliver Ellison, Worthy, and the brother’s biological parents. Worthy and the brother ended up in foster care,” Megan said. “Maybe there was a reason the Ellisons didn’t adopt the brother. He could have been violent and the family was afraid of him.”

“I wonder why they didn’t adopt Worthy?” Sierra asked. “She seems innocent in all of this.”

“Possibly. We really need to speak with her more to know the family history,” Hannah said. “We’re missing something.”

Cooper’s eyes widened. “Like maybe Oliver really has a brother and possibly sisters. After the biological parents were out of the picture for whatever reason, Oliver was adopted but the rest of the siblings were not.” “That would certainly make the brother feel unworthy. He and Worthy—and any other siblings—may have all been at the same orphanage,” Hannah said. “We’ll need a last name to locate them.”

“The initials on the sketch Ellison drew were P.A. It stands to reason the brother's last name begins with an A.” Zeke grabbed his laptop. “I'm going to see if I can locate any orphanages near Pottsville. Maybe we can have something break our way before these two decide to take another innocent life.”

CHAPTER TWENTY-FOUR

food around on the plate. "This is your favorite meal." hy aren't you eating?" he asked, watching her push her He'd stopped by her house unexpectedly because he sensed something in her voice when he called her.

She didn't look at him. "I'm not really hungry. I think I'm coming down with something." As if to emphasize the deceit, she coughed.

"That's too bad. And it's your favorite." His tone turned hard. Why was she lying to him? They shared everything with each other.

He carried their plates to the sink and dumped the wasted food down the disposal while trying to harness his anger. "How's work?" he asked once he'd returned to the table.

"Good." She grabbed a pack of cigarettes and lit one up. A nervous habit.

His mouth thinned distastefully. How many times had he asked her not to smoke around him? "Put it out."

She immediately removed the cigarette from her mouth and stubbed it out. "Sorry."

"What are you so nervous about?" She only smoked when stressed by work or by one deadbeat boyfriend after another.

"Nothing. Just work." The fib rolled off her tongue with the confidence of someone who had plenty of practice.

"I thought you said work was good?"

She finally looked at him. "It is. Mostly." She blew out a cigarettescented breath his way. "Just my new boss. He's being a real jerk."

She worked at a diner that had changed hands multiple times. He decided to humor her for a bit. "Why is he being a jerk?" It was always something. He'd done his best to be patient with her through the years because he, of all people, understood the difficulties she faced in adjusting to the world after what they'd gone through, and she was the last of his family.

"He has it out for me. He told me I'd have to start working the latenight shift from here on out. You know there are only losers who come in at that time. Most only want coffee. They don't tip. It's awful."

Same story he'd heard for years. They were out to get her.

"Quit. You have some money saved right?"

Her gaze dropped to the ashtray. She had a nasty heroin habit that she'd promised she'd beat.

He grabbed her arm and pushed her shirt sleeve up. Track marks spoke the truth even if she couldn't.

"I'm sorry, Petie. I tried." Tears filled her eyes.

He let her go and paced the tiny kitchen of her trailer. This weakness was something he didn't understand.

"You know I tried." She tailed him around as he walked.

He turned on her and unleashed his fury. "Do I? And how would I know that? You haven't been able to string more than a day or two of sobriety together since I found you again."

She flinched then began bawling at his rebuke. In the past it had always worked. But he had other things to consider now. At one time, he'd planned to make her part of his immortals. They talked of being together forever. He told her about the sisters he'd give her—like the ones they once had.

"Go wash your face."

She wiped her nose on the back of her sleeve. "We're okay, aren't we, Petie?"

He forced a smile. "Yes, we're okay. Go ahead. We'll have some ice cream."

She laughed and hugged his neck.

Once she'd gone, he found her phone and checked it. She'd called two numbers. Both of them he recognized. Her betrayal sealed her fate. He scooped ice cream and shoved aside what must be done.

She padded down the hallway. "What flavor did you get?"

"What do you think?" He held out the bowl of chocolate ice cream.

She clapped her hands. "Oh, thank you, thank you."

"Let's sit." He returned to his seat across from hers.

"How are our plans coming?" She shoved a spoonful of ice cream into her mouth.

At one time, they'd been on the same page. Getting a family together that would last forever. She'd let her weakness for drugs cloud her thinking. He'd thought he could save her. But now he saw she was unworthy of saving.

The knife in his pocket waited to be used. He gazed at her, taking in every inch of her face. Before the drugs she'd been beautiful. Years of abuse had destroyed her beauty. Now, the only ones who sniffed around were just as messed up as she was.

She caught him staring. "Why are you looking at me like that? Do I have something on my face?" She rubbed her hand over her mouth and chin.

He chuckled. "You missed it. Here, let me." He rose and went over to her. She froze when he pushed her stringy dark hair aside. He placed his hand around her neck.

"W-what are you doing?"

He removed the knife. "Taking care of a problem. Goodbye, little sister. I'm sorry, but you are no longer worthy."

Before she could react, he slid the knife over her throat, ending all ability to talk. He would spare her the rest of what he did to those he found unworthy. She was, after all, his sister.

He stood back and watched her grab for her throat and try to stop the flow of blood while her frantic eyes held his, a single tear slipping down her face.

"Don't fight it. Let death come."

But she did. She fought harder in death than she ever had in life. She flopped over on her side and then down onto the floor as the last of her life left her body.

Once she was gone, he knelt beside her. "I'm sorry it had to end like this." He closed her eyes, careful to avoid touching her blood.

He pulled gloves from his pocket and went about wiping any fingerprints he'd left. Not that it would matter. He wasn't in the system. But she was. She'd been busted many times for drugs and selling herself to buy drugs.

The trailer was set on a couple of acres in the woods. She had no neighbors to spy. No record of him in connection to her. Still, he searched the house from top to bottom. If she'd called the police and spoken to *him*, then it stood to reason she planned to betray him.

Once he'd made sure the place was clean, he wrapped her lifeless body in the dirty living room rug and carried her out to the car, but not before writing one word. Eventually her absence would be reported. They'd come looking for her. And when they did, he wanted them to see what her fate had been. Below the word, he added something just for her. Snitch.

CHAPTER TWENTY-FIVE

Hannah got up from the table and walked to the windows, reflecting on the day. They'd been at it for hours and were no closer to the answers they needed than before.

Worthy hadn't answered any calls. Unless they could locate her another way, Hannah believed she would prove to be a dead end.

Cooper materialized beside her a welcomed relief from her chaotic thoughts. "Want to take a walk outside to get some fresh air?"

They'd been stuck inside the conference room going over different aspects of the case.

"I'd love to stretch my legs." She grabbed her coat and bag and stepped outside to a day quickly fading. The cold air invigorated her. "How are you holding up?"

He slipped her hand in his. She froze for a moment then interlocked their fingers.

"I'm still in shock after hearing my father is alive."

They headed past the hotel portico. "There's no indication your father's been killing since he got out of prison before these current cases. I wonder what triggered him?" Hannah's attention went to the passing cars on the road in front of the hotel.

"I think finding that answer will be the key to unraveling what's really going on."

She looked his way. "You mean who the second player is. If he's Oliver's brother, then where's he been?"

"Exactly." Cooper pointed to a coffeehouse next door. "Want to grab some coffee?"

She chuckled. "Sure. It's not like we haven't consumed enough lately."

He laughed, too. "Yeah, right." Still, they went inside and found a booth. The business was almost completely empty.

They ordered coffee and pie.

"Why don't we talk about something else? Anything but the case."
The details of it swam in her head, getting jumbled together.

"Deal." He glanced around the establishment. "How's your mother?"

He was trying. For two people whose whole life revolved around the
job, finding a topic of conversation other than it wasn't so easy.

"She's okay. After Ellie passed, she worried every day. She stayed
with me for a while until I couldn't handle it any longer." She shrugged.
"We've never been close really. I think having a child who was sick all
the time took its toll on her. It wasn't easy." Their coffee and pie arrived.

"That had to be hard," he said dumping sugar into his coffee. He
obviously felt sorry for her after everything she'd been through.

"It made me stronger, and I had Zeke. He never let me down when
others did."

"He's a good guy." Cooper dug into his apple pie with ice cream on
top. "This is good. Want some?"

She remembered the many times when they'd worked a case in the
past, they'd ordered food and ended up sharing it.

Hannah tried the pie and closed her eyes. "You're right. It is good. So
is the chocolate silk." She pushed the plate over for him to try it.

"I'm not sure which I like the best." Cooper sipped his coffee. "Ever
wonder what our lives would be like if we both were normal?"

She almost snorted her coffee. "Thanks a lot."

"You know what I mean."

She did. They'd both gone through something that would break
many. She thought having a heart transplant so young was awful. But
watching your father kill your mother and then having to shoot him to keep
from dying . . .

"Tell me about your life with the Delaneys. They sound like nice
people."

He smiled when he talked about them. "They saved my life. I can't
imagine what I'd be like if I hadn't been adopted by them." He finished off
the last of his pie. "They're an older couple who remind me a lot of my
great-grandparents. They moved me away and sheltered me from the fallout
of my father's crimes. I had no idea until after I'd left home that he'd died."

She sipped her coffee. "Was it hard hearing he'd been convicted of
all those murders?"

He shook his head. "Not really. By then, the hate I had for him taking my mother overpowered the love I once felt. I think I realized the person I thought Oliver was didn't exist."

From what they'd uncovered so far it seemed to prove true.

Cooper's phone alerted to a message. "Doesn't look like ERT found any matches for the DNA yet. They have mine on file to match it against. If this mystery person was my father's brother, shouldn't it make a hit?"

She thought as much. "Perhaps he wasn't your father's biological brother. After all, the Embalmer persona refers to his victims as family."

"True."

The waitress brought over their ticket. Hannah grabbed it. "My treat." She reached inside her bag for her wallet and froze.

"Hannah?"

She vaguely registered him saying her name, yet she couldn't respond because of the note lying in her purse. Her breathing came rapidly. She struggled not to hyperventilate.

"Hannah, what's wrong?" Cooper slipped into the booth beside her.

She pointed because words wouldn't come.

The pale-blue parchment paper had been left in her purse. The only time she'd left the bag unattended was during their search of Cooper's great-grandparents' home.

Cooper brought the folded paper out. He opened it and read the words.

Beloved, now that I've found your heart, I'll never let you go. Soon, you'll be mine again as before. Now and always.

"What is this?" He looked at her but all she could do was stare at the paper. This one was different. This time the writer mentioned her heart in particular. That couldn't be an accident.

"Hey, it's going to be okay." He gathered her close and held her while she struggled to regain her composure. Hannah couldn't stop shaking. She'd faced down many killers in her time with BAU, yet this person stalking her scared the daylights out of her.

"Everything alright here?" The waitress noticed Hannah's distress and came to investigate.

"She's fine." Cooper paid the bill. After a moment of doubt, the waitress stepped away.

"Who gave you this?" Cooper tried again once she stopped shaking. She pulled away and struggled to find words to tell him the nightmare she'd been living with that had everything to do with her dreams.

CHAPTER TWENTY-SIX

As Hannah's story unfolded, Cooper forgot all about his father. He couldn't believe she hadn't told him about the notes before now. "We need to let the others know."

She shook her head repeatedly. "You can't. They'll take me off the case."

His eyes widened. "Hannah, your life's in danger. Whoever this person is, he came into our hotel and left the message while we all slept. He slipped this into your purse while we were at the house. He's got a fixation with you that seems to be getting darker. This could be connected to the Embalmer case."

She wiped her face. "It isn't."

"You don't know that for certain."

"I do. In my gut I do."

He clasped her hand. "Look, I know you don't want to share this with everyone, but I promise it will be okay. I'll talk to Jack."

She searched his face. "You will?"

He smiled, yet he couldn't help but wonder if her stalker were related to Embalmer.

She told him about her uneasiness when in Nolan Lewis's presence. "He gave me the creeps."

He noticed the waitress watching them still. "Let's get out of here." He stood, and she slipped into her coat. They headed back to the hotel.

"We checked Lewis before, and he appeared clean. Maybe he's using an alias." Cooper wondered if they could try to get prints off the notes or if the stalker wore gloves. If ERT could retrieve a print, they might find a lead to who was stalking her.

Cooper put his arm around her as they crossed the parking lot. They were almost to the hotel when a car grabbed his attention behind them. It appeared to be following them. Small and white . . . like the one Lewis had driven.

Cooper whipped around. Saw Lewis behind the wheel. "Go inside. Now, Hannah."

She ran toward the entrance. Once she was safe, Cooper started toward Lewis's car.

He quickly whipped the vehicle around and floored it, shooting across the parking lot without regard for other cars or pedestrians.

Cooper raced toward the Armada and jumped inside. Hannah, who had been waiting under the portico instead of going inside, got in next to him.

"What are you doing?" He fired the engine.

"Going with you. This person is coming after me, Cooper."

And he was getting away. He shoved the gearshift into Drive and started after Lewis. Cooper was forced to slow down to miss a car pulling out in front of them. As soon as the car cleared, he headed for the road. "He went right." Cooper turned and maneuvered through the traffic as best he could. "Do you see him?"

Hannah leaned forward and searched their surroundings. "No, I don't." Her cell phone buzzed a message. "It's Jack. They must have seen us leave." She called Jack and told him what happened. "We're searching for the car now."

"Be careful, Hannah. This guy is clearly infatuated with you, and I have a feeling there's more to the story than what you've told." Jack's tone held disappointment.

"You're right. I'll tell you everything once we return." She waited for a response that didn't come before she ended the call.

Cooper searched sideroads on his side while Hannah did the same. After they'd traveled a couple of miles, the truth became clear. Lewis had escaped.

"That's it. He's gone." He made the safest U-turn he could and headed back to the hotel. "There's more to Lewis than what we uncovered. We need to find out who he really is and what he wants from you."

They reached the hotel to find everyone waiting for them.

"What on earth happened?" Sierra asked while giving Hannah a hug.

Cooper looked Hannah's way. "Let's go inside, and we'll explain everything we know."

He kept close to Hannah because he cared about her, and he'd seen how difficult it had been for her to share with him. They were a close-knit team and yet some secrets were best left hidden. He certainly understood as much.

He slipped his hand in hers, hoping to give her encouragement as the story slowly unfolded.

Zeke was the most upset. "Why didn't you tell me you were being threatened?"

"I didn't want to worry you. You've been so worried about me since Ellie died. I wanted to spare you."

Zeke tugged his sister into his arms. "Don't ever do that again. You're my family. I want to know what's going on in your life."

She slowly nodded.

"Where are the notes?" Jack asked.

Hannah pulled them from her bag using her gloves. "I've handled them, carefully, but I handled them."

"I have too. Just the last one. Briefly when I unfolded the note to read it," Cooper added.

"Here's an evidence bag." Megan handed her husband the bag.

Jack placed the notes inside. "I'm calling Bob." He stepped away to make the call.

"I can't believe you had a heart transplant so young." Sierra seemed surprised. She was the only one who didn't know about the transplant.

"It's not something I like to talk about," Hannah told her.

Sierra hugged her close. "I get that. But I'm here too if you ever want to unload."

Hannah smiled. "I'll keep that in mind."

"Bob's coming over. He'll work from here to see if we can get any viable prints."

And if they did find out Lewis's real name, and it was the person who claimed to be his father's brother, would he be able to stop his father and uncle from taking her from him?

The thought of losing Hannah ripped his guts out. He wasn't willing to face that possible reality, certainly not to a monster from his past or some sick individual stalking her. He loved her. Wouldn't lose her. Not like that. Not to a monster.

"I found something."

All eyes turned to Zeke.

"It took some digging, but I followed Jane's lead about your adoptive grandparents and found this." He turned the laptop around. "Fern Ellison has a sister named Suzanne Moriarty."

"You're kidding?" Cooper couldn't believe it. "There was no mention of her in the obits."

"No, you're right. I don't know if they had a falling out or if it was an oversight, but she's still alive and lives near Jonestown." Zeke pulled up the address.

"I want to speak with her. Do you have a phone number?"

"Give me a second . . ." Zeke typed some keys and squinted at the screen. "A landline. No record of a cell."

"That's odd." Cooper typed the number into his phone and waited through five rings before it went to voicemail. He identified himself and asked Suzanne to call him back.

Megan stood and held her lower back. "It's late. We all need to get some rest. Let's start fresh in the morning."

Everyone but Hannah and Cooper left. Cooper tried to urge her to get some rest.

Hannah paced the conference room. "I'm too keyed up." She stopped walking. "Do you think this is just some sicko playing games with me, or is it somehow connected to this case?" She grabbed a water. "Want some?"

He declined. "As much as I don't need it, I'm going for coffee even though I think I have more caffeine in my veins than blood at this point." She laughed. Hannah poured him a cup and returned to her seat.

"To answer your question, I think this is separate. Definitely Lewis or whoever he really is."

"What about the company he works for? We talked to them, right?"

Cooper started to say yes, but then hesitated. "We must have. He checked out."

"Or did he?" Hannah wondered if Lewis had manipulated the record somehow.

"Let's find out." He looked up Empire Windows and called the number.

"Hello." He sat up straighter, surprised someone answered at that time of day.

"Yes, this is Cooper Delaney." He identified himself as FBI and switched the call to speaker.

"Agent Delaney. We're actually closed. I'm just catching up on some paperwork. Can you call back tomorrow?"

"I'm sorry, it can't wait. This is important."

The woman sighed her annoyance. "Fine. How can I help you?"

"I'm calling about one of your employees. Nolan Lewis. I'd like to ask you some questions about him."

"Let me see if I can help you. I'm not in human resources." The sound of keys being punched. "Well, this is strange. I don't see an employee by that name. Are you sure of the name?"

"Yes I am."

"Hang on a second."

Cooper's stomach tightened as he listened to the hold music. How had Lewis managed to doctor his employment history to pass an FBI detailed search?

The woman came back on the line. "Agent Delaney, I think we have the mix-up. We had a Luis Noland who worked for us for a while, but he is no longer employed here."

"Did he quit or was he fired?" Cooper had a feeling he knew the answer.

"Mr. Noland was let go." Her tone became even more guarded.

"Ma'am, we're investigating a stalking incident. Luis Noland might have information about the case. I need everything you can tell me about him."

"He was fired because he appeared to be using his route to track down women he claimed to have a relationship with."

Beloved, now that I've found you again. I will never let you go. You will be with me soon. Now and always. "When was this?"

"Six months earlier."

"I need you to send me his file." Cooper gave her his email address.

"I'll do it now."

"Thank you." Cooper ended the call, reeling with shock. The cover Noland had created for himself appeared squeaky clean.

"Wow." Hannah stared at her laptop screen. "You're not going to believe this. Luis Noland killed his wife around nineteen years ago."

"You're kidding?" Cooper came around and pulled out the chair beside her. "He didn't go to prison?"

She shook her head. "No. He was committed to a psychiatric hospital. He's been out for almost a year."

"Is there an address for Noland now?" Cooper waited while she searched for the information. "The same as he listed under the Noland identity." She put the address into Google Maps and realized it was an empty building. "A dead end."

"What about the car? It was registered to Lewis. Did he finance it?"

Another search had her shaking her head. "He paid cash."

"He covered all his bases. What's his connection to you? You two have never met, right?"

Hannah immediately confirmed they hadn't. She focused hard on Noland's image. "I know him, Cooper. I don't know how yet, but of one thing I'm certain. I know Luis Noland somehow."

CHAPTER TWENTYSEVEN

He wanted to know everything he could about her. He'd been watching her. Following her when she wasn't aware. She was tough as nails and could handle herself in any dangerous situation, and yet she hadn't thought twice about him. They'd passed by each other several times. Once, she'd even said excuse me when she accidently brushed into him. He could still smell her perfume on that shirt.

It was almost time to make her the next beauty. A sister and part of his distinguished family.

Mentor had someone else in mind. A schoolteacher who worked at the school in Grand Island. Mentor had sent him into town today to watch the teacher. That wasn't going to happen. He had someone much better in mind. He'd decided to humor Mentor for the time being while he plotted how to rid himself of the man he no longer found useful.

He'd watched his beauty go to the coffeehouse near their hotel. She and her partner. The incident the previous day had everyone spooked. He waited a few minutes before going inside. He slipped into the booth a few feet away from her. That perfume she wore wafted his way. He closed his eyes and drank in the scent.

Footsteps stopped next to his booth. He tamped down his anger. A fifty-something waitress stood beside his table with a menu.

"I'll just have coffee to go, please."

She eyed his gloves. His hoodie and watch cap—sunglasses—that covered his identity. She continued to study him for a long moment before making a harrumphing sound as she left.

Disgusting woman. She would never be worthy.

He pretended to study his sugar packet and listened to her and her partner talk. What happened the day before was a great deal of their conversation. She was talking about him.

He smiled and imagined all the conversations they'd have in the future.

Her partner received a call. He excused himself and stepped outside.

Perfect. He had time to sneak little glimpses of her while she studied her menu.

"Here you go." The waitress plopped the coffee cup down on the table loudly.

She turned her head slightly to look at him. He smiled. A moment or two passed while she tried to place him and couldn't. She returned to perusing the menu. Her partner came back inside.

The waitress moved to their table to take their orders.

Stupid woman.

He dumped sugar packets into his coffee and pocketed their wrappers. Best not to leave any evidence behind. He dropped enough money on the table to pay for the coffee, making sure not to leave the rude waitress a tip, then he slipped out of the establishment and returned to his car with a smile on his face.

Tonight. Yes, tonight would be the perfect time to claim her for his own.

He drove slowly by the business, catching another look at her. So pretty. She would stand up to Mentor for him, he knew it. Perhaps he'd even get her to help find other family members before he made her eternal. Oh, what fun they'd have together.

CHAPTER TWENTYEIGHT

Suzanne Moriarty hadn't called them back. Still, Hannah believed they might be able to convince her to speak with them if they showed up at her house.

Megan remained at the hotel, joined by Detective Siegler and her partner, on loan from the Grand Island PD. They'd continue to comb through the mountain of information pouring in as the case continued to grow more confusing.

With Zeke taking over as driver, Hannah and Cooper volunteered to sit in the third-row seating of the Suburban.

Suzanne Moriarty was almost seventy-nine by now. She'd never married. Had no remaining family left.

As much as Hannah tried to keep her focus on the Embalmer case, all she could think about was Luis Noland. He'd killed his wife. Had been sentenced to a mental hospital for years, and now that he was out he was stalking Hannah. She wanted to understand why. She'd left a message for the psychiatrist who had treated Noland at the facility.

"You okay?" Cooper asked quietly. She turned away from watching the countryside pass by.

"Just thinking about Noland. How long has he been following me and why?"

He reached for her hand. "He mentioned your heart. I'm hoping his doctor will be able to shed some light on that."

"Me too."

"Looks like this is it." Zeke pulled up beside an older house in a neighborhood that had seen better days.

They got out and started for the porch.

"Cooper, you should probably take the lead. You have somewhat of a connection to her." Jack stood next to the peeling green door.

Cooper leaned forward and knocked a couple of times. Not a sound came from inside.

"Is she home?" Hannah stepped from the porch and looked at the side of the house. There wasn't a garage, and no car was parked nearby.

"Maybe she no longer drives," Sierra said as she followed Hannah. Since she was older, that would make sense.

Hannah shook her head. At times, she felt positively old around Sierra. The woman was twenty-five but had more energy than Hannah ever had.

Cooper knocked again. This time there was a response. "I'm coming. Hold your horses."

Zeke chuckled. "Sounds like we've got a live one."

The door opened. A frail-looking woman, with thinning white hair and dressed in a housecoat, eyed them all suspiciously. "What do you want? I'm not interested in buying anything, and I already know Jesus."

Cooper brought out his ID. "We're not soliciting. Are you Suzanne Moriarty?"

That he knew her name only seemed to make her more suspicious. "That's right. What does the FBI want with me? I haven't robbed a bank or killed anyone."

"We'd like to ask you some questions about your sister, Fern."

Suzanne wasn't expecting this. "Fern? She's been dead for years." Yet the show of emotion on her creased face confirmed she still missed her sister.

Cooper asked her if she remembered Fern and Greg's adopted son, Oliver.

Suzanne's hand flew to her mouth. "Oh, dear me."

Cooper glanced at Hannah before telling Suzanne he was Oliver's son. "Do you mind if we come inside? We'd like to talk to you about what you know about Oliver's past."

The older woman stepped back to let them inside. She directed them to the living room. The house was small but neat. Hannah sat beside Cooper while the rest of the team found seats. A woodstove burned fiercely, making the room feel like a sauna. Hannah removed her coat and rolled up the sleeves of her sweater.

"You look just like him," Suzanne claimed. Cooper flinched. It wasn't a compliment. "I heard he killed several people. What happened to him?"

Cooper laid it all out for her. "He escaped from prison. He's killing again."

Suzanne didn't appear surprised. "I told Fern he was trouble. Even when he was a child, he was evil."

Hannah leaned forward. "What do you mean?"

"I mean, I think he killed them."

Nothing prepared Hannah for the accusation.

"The police report claims Greg killed Fern and then himself," Cooper challenged.

"I know what the police said, but I'm telling you that boy did it."

"How can you be sure, ma'am?" Jack asked. "According to the police, Oliver was away at college."

She made a derisive snort. "He was always in trouble in school. He'd gotten suspended several times. He used college as an excuse."

Cooper asked her if they could go back to the beginning. "Oliver was six when he was adopted by your sister and her husband. Do you remember how they got connected with Oliver? We haven't been able to find out anything about his past."

"The devil's spawn," she spat out. "Fern never told me where he came from. She said there was a family who couldn't afford to keep him and they gave him up for adoption to them."

"They knew the family?" Hannah pressed.

"I think so. Fern did mention something to me once that I thought was strange. She said they had several kids. I got the impression that they were troubled people. They'd abused the children, according to Fern."

That might be the foundation for Oliver's mental illness. On a whim, Hannah asked if there were any documents from the family left.

Suzanne shook her head. "Not a thing. Oliver cleaned the house out and then sold it. I had asked for some of my sister's personal things, but he wouldn't let me have them."

He was making sure there would be no way to find out about his past.

Hannah believed it was because there was something hidden there.

"But there was one thing . . ."

Hannah focused on the woman.

"Fern brought it over a few days before her death. I'll get it." She struggled to stand.

"Do you need some help?" Hannah asked.

Suzanne waved her off. "I'm not helpless." She disappeared down the hall.

"He got rid of everything that could tie him to his brother and family so that we couldn't find them. I wonder what happened to their parents. Was what my dad told Isobel true, and the brother killed their father?" Cooper ran a hand across his neck.

"They were obviously not fit to care for their children. I wonder how many there were?" Was the monster that Oliver turned into formed when he was just a child? Or was he born that way?

"Here you go." Suzanne came back into the room carrying a small metal box. "I looked through it, but nothing made any sense to me." "May I?" Cooper asked, and she gave her consent.

"You can take it with you."

Cooper opened the box. A handful of old photos lay inside. He brought out the first one. A house in the woods with several kids playing in front. "You have no idea who these people are?"

Hannah could see that she did. "Who are they?"

Suzanne riffled through the photos and brought one out. "This is Oliver." She handed the photo to Hannah. A young boy around five stared at the camera. His eyes were cold and dark even back then.

Hannah handed the photo to Cooper and examined the one of the house. One of the kids playing out front was Oliver. Were the others his brothers and sisters?

"There are three boys. Four girls." Oliver had deemed four women worthy when he'd bricked them up in the basement. Hannah reached for the next photo. It showed a woman who appeared to be in her early thirties, looking terrified of the person behind the camera. She passed it to Cooper.

"There's a name written on the back of this photo." Cooper had flipped it over. "Elizabeth. No last name."

Hannah searched the rest of the photos. "Nothing is written on these."

Cooper's attention went back to the photo of the house. "There's a car in the background here." He handed it to Zeke. "Can you make out the plate?"

Zeke held it close. "I think it's a Pennsylvania plate. I'll run this through the FBI's photo processing program to see if I can make the number more visible. From there, I'll see if I can trace the owner of the vehicle. It won't be easy."

If Zeke could somehow trace the car to its owner, perhaps they could find the names of Oliver's real parents.

Hannah handed Suzanne her card. "If you think of anything else, please give me a call. Thank you for your time."

Suzanne walked them to the door. "If you find out what really happened to my sister, I'd like to know."

"I will give you a call with whatever we discover," Hannah promised.

"You drive," Zeke handed Cooper the keys to the SUV. "I'm digging into this plate number."

As they headed back to the hotel, Zeke went to work on tracking the plate. Thanks to the FBI's technology, by the time they reached Grand Island, Zeke had the names of Oliver's real parents.

"Bruce and Elizabeth Albertson. They lived near Sugar Grove, Pennsylvania."

"Lived? Are they . . . ?" Hannah asked. She thought about Isobel's claim that Oliver's brother had killed their father.

"Not sure. They moved from Sugar Grove several decades earlier."

Jack parked the SUV under the portico. "Do we know the names of the other children?"

"Not yet. I'll keep digging."

They got out and returned to the hotel. Hannah glanced toward the diner where she and Cooper had coffee the day before and shivered. How did Noland think he knew her? She checked her phone. Still nothing from the doctor.

"I have good news on Isobel," Megan told them. "She's been upgraded from critical. Her doctor believes she'll survive the attack, although she's still not awake."

"Thank God for that." Hannah had been worried about Isobel. She noticed Detective Jordan seated at the table. "Where's Detective Siegler?"

"She had to run home for a second. She should be back soon."

"Anything new here?" Sierra asked, flipping through the stacks of papers on the table.

Megan told her no.

"Well, this is interesting." The excitement in Zeke's tone confirmed he had something big.

"You found the names of the other children?" Hannah knew her brother well enough to be certain he wouldn't stop until he had them.

"I did." Everyone gathered around. "Looks like Oliver was the only one adopted as far as I can tell. The records are sketchy from back then."

Hannah noticed he'd tapped into social services records. "Apparently, the Albertson family moved to the Rochester area from Sugar Grove. Elizabeth had a connection to the Ellisons. She cleaned house for them a couple of days a week."

"You're kidding?" Sierra looked over his shoulder. "You get all that from social services?"

Zeke smiled up at her. "I did. There's a note in Oliver's file. The Ellisons requested to foster Oliver. They said he came with his mother from time to time and they'd developed a connection."

"That explains the adoption." Cooper pulled out the chair next to Zeke. "The family appeared fairly well off. They didn't want to take any of the other children?"

Zeke shook his head. "No mention of a reason why."

"What were the other children's names?" Hannah wondered if one of the boys had the initials P.A.

"The girls are Lucy, the oldest at thirteen then. Missy, nine. Callie, seven. Tonya, two."

"Wait—Callie and Tonya were two of the names Oliver displayed over his worthy victims, correct?" Hannah remembered those names as being very specific.

"That's right. He was naming the worthy victims after his sisters, apparently. Anyway, the boys' names are James, who was five. Oliver, six, and Pete, four."

"P.A.—Pete Albertson." Hannah grabbed the sketchbook from the stack of documents on the table and flipped through it until she found the one of the man Oliver claimed to be his brother. "This is Pete—his brother."

"This is our first solid lead in a while." Cooper leaned his elbows on the table. "Where's Pete now?"

"Don't know. I'll see if I can find out," Zeke told him.

Sierra pulled out a chair next to Zeke. "I'll help you search. Let me take the girls. If we can find one of them, perhaps they can shed some light on Oliver and Pete."

"I'll see if I can locate James." Alex pulled his laptop closer and started the search.

Hannah grabbed bottled waters for her and Cooper. Before she opened the cap, a message came in on her phone. She read through it. "It's Doctor Hoffman. He wants to talk in person. He says he has news on Noland we should hear."

Cooper set his bottle down. "Where's he at?"

Hannah noticed the address. "About forty-five minutes from here."

Cooper glanced back at the team. "They have everything covered here. Let's go see what the doctor has to say."

CHAPTER TWENTY-NINE

"I need to tell you something . . ."

Dread cloaked him like a coat as he put the Armada into Drive. "Go ahead."

"I saw a photo of Noland's wife in his records." She swallowed several times. "Cooper, I recognized her."

He shot her a look. "How?"

"From my dreams . . ."

He prepared for the other shoe to drop. "You'd better explain." His hands actually shook on the wheel.

"Off and on since I received the transplant, but lately more often, I've had dreams—vivid dreams of a woman. Brenda Noland—she's the woman from my dreams, and, yes, I realize how crazy that sounds."

He kept his doubts to himself. "What are the dreams about?"

"She—Brenda is terrified of her husband. He beats her. She's afraid of leaving him." There were tears in her eyes. "She feels so helpless. I think Brenda knew he would kill her one day."

"You think you're experiencing these dreams because you have her heart?" He tried not to show his doubts, but it sounded like a bunch of hocus-pocus to him.

"They're called cellular memories, and there have been many documented cases of transplant patients having them."

He wanted to believe her, but Cooper was a black-and-white guy. And this was definitely a gray area.

He let the subject drop and didn't miss her disappointment. "What do we know about Doctor Archibald Hoffman?" Cooper asked as they headed for the interstate.

Hannah had spoken briefly to Dr. Hoffman, who had a lot to say. "The hospital where Noland was incarcerated fired Hoffman."

Cooper whipped his head her way. "What? Why?"

"The doctor says it was because he didn't go along with what was being suggested." Hannah shrugged.

"And that was . . . ?" Cooper did his best to squelch the sinking feeling in his gut. They desperately needed a break on finding Noland.

"He said the board of trustees at Brookhaven wanted Hoffman to medicate, treat, and release, regardless of the inmate's condition, to allow for more patients, which meant more government funding. Hoffman mentioned he warned them about releasing Noland. Said he understood the man was violent and a sociopath that showed no signs of rehabilitation. The board didn't listen to his recommendations."

Cooper glanced out the windshield as they entered a quiet suburban neighborhood and tried to understand why anyone would okay the release of a violent person like their killer obviously was. "You're kidding. Can he substantiate any of those accusations?"

Hannah threw him an "oh, please" look. "Nope. They covered their tracks too well. The good doctor had a long list of grievances against him by the time they fired him. I checked them out. The worst being that Doctor Hoffman's a drug addict. He'd gotten caught prescribing narcotics to himself. Hoffman's not exactly credible, but he's all we have. I'm hoping he can shed some light on Noland's friends, hangouts—anything that might help us find him."

Cooper ran a hand across his bleary eyes. "Great. This case keeps getting better and better."

"It's the one on the left," Hannah told him.

Doctor Archibald Hoffman's house was one of the more affluent ones in the neighborhood.

"Not bad for a fired drug addict." Cooper let out a low whistle as he pulled in front of the two-story red-brick Georgian. "Was he selling the scripts?"

"Not according to him. There's nothing I found that backs that up. But then, the information available is slim."

Cooper got out of the Armada and waited for Hannah. He wished he had more confidence in this visit, but the doctor's drug allegations hung in his head. If the case came to trial, any decent defense attorney would shred the good doctor's testimony to bits.

As they approached a small flagstone porch, Hannah rang the doorbell, and they waited in silence.

The front door opened and a slightly built middle-aged man with glasses pushed high on his forehead appeared puzzled by their appearance. As if they'd interrupted an afternoon perusing of a book.

"May I help you?"

"Doctor Hoffman, I'm Hannah London and this is Cooper Delaney. We're with the FBI." When the confusion didn't clear, she added, "I called you about one of your patients. Luis Noland."

"Oh, yes." The doctor cast a curious look Cooper's way.

"May we come in?"

The gray-haired man stepped back and let them inside. "Of course, of course. I was in the middle of reviewing some cases."

Cooper gave Hannah a "what's going on?" look.

Doctor Hoffman saw their exchange and grinned. "Ah, your partner told you the reason they fired me from Brookhaven. Well, I'm working in the private sector now."

"I see." Cooper couldn't believe the man would be permitted to practice until completely cleared of the charges against him.

"I will be cleared, I assure you," he said as if reading Cooper's thoughts. "I'm in the process of suing Brookhaven for wrongful termination." The doctor showed them to a small office and indicated they should have a seat.

"With all due respect, doctor, if you didn't fight the charges against you when they fired you, why are you suing now?" Cooper had to ask the obvious. According to Hannah, the doctor had been fired more than a year earlier.

"Because I wanted out of that horrible place. I'd seen things that no human being should ever see. When I brought the list of wrongdoings to the board, they told me I was overreacting. That I should keep my mouth closed."

"So, you're saying they fired you to keep you quiet. It must have been some list," Cooper challenged.

"Oh, it was. The list was long indeed. Patient abuse. Over-prescribing drugs. Falsifying patient records to make it look as if they were getting better when in truth that wasn't the case."

"Is that what happened with Luis Noland?"

"Oh my, yes," the doctor acknowledged with a grim shake of his head. "They pushed me to recommend that he even be free to work in the administration office. As a trial run."

That didn't make sense to Cooper. "Really? Even knowing he'd murdered his wife?"

The doctor lowered his head. "Our goal is to help our patients overcome their disease and live a productive life again, Agent Delaney." He glanced at them. "As I said, he's good at fooling people. He had everyone else there fooled. But not me. Never me."

According to what they'd discovered, Noland had tracked down women he believed to have had his wife's heart and slaughtered them. "What more can you tell us about Luis Noland?"

Doctor Hoffman hesitated. "As I told Agent London on the phone, my identity must remain secret. No one can suspect I was the one who spoke to you concerning this patient. I'm filing a wrongful termination lawsuit against the institute. If they found out I talked to you . . ."

"Doctor, we don't care about outing you to anyone. We need your help. Noland's been stalking Agent London because of her heart transplant. I believe he's stepping up his attempts to get to her. Whatever you choose to do regarding the lawsuit is your decision."

The doctor expelled a heavy sigh. "Those foolish people. Those foolish, foolish people. I tried to tell them what I believed him capable of, and what did they do? Replaced me with an incompetent yes-man and drummed up false charges against me to make me seem disreputable."

Hoffman shook his head. "You see, I was the original psychiatrist assigned to Noland's case when he arrived at the institute. From our first session together, I saw the potential for much evil in him. I warned the board if they let him free, he'd not only kill again, he'd do it repeatedly. The man is a sociopath. He has no conscience, no sense of right or wrong. Frankly, he scared the daylights out of me."

Hannah had been busy scribbling notes. She stopped long enough to add, "Obviously the court agreed with you when they sentenced him to Brookhaven. I've read the court records. He became so deranged the judge recommended Luis Noland never be released."

The doctor nodded. "Yes. They had to sedate him on high doses of Desyrel Trazodone for a month before I was able to see him, much less get him to talk to me somewhat rationally. When he did, all he talked about was his wife. He was like an injured animal. He spoke as if she were still alive. I tried to get him to accept the fact that he'd killed her and, hopefully, come to some type of terms with it, but he insisted she was still living. He seemed to think she talked to him."

"If Noland thought his wife was still alive, then how did he explain her organs being used for transplants?" Cooper asked.

The doctor gave them a weary smile. "I don't know. He is a very intelligent man. When he was allowed to work in the office . . . I soon discovered he'd been using my medical license to check out medical records. When I confronted him with this, he told me he needed to find out where they'd taken his wife."

Cooper exchanged a skeptical look with Hannah.

"Oh, yes," the doctor confirmed. "Well, needless to say, after that he was no longer allowed in the office. It was at that time I started receiving thinly veiled threats from him during our sessions. As a precaution, I dug around in his background. I wanted some idea what I was dealing with. Just how sick this man was. What I learned scared me more than any other patient I'd dealt with. Luis Noland worked as a carpenter before he murdered his wife. After getting fired from numerous jobs, working construction was all he found."

The doctor's expression grew serious. "I discovered a record of where he'd applied to the Naval Academy when he was young. They did an IQ test, and the man was a genius. Most colleges are anxious to recruit such a candidate, but the Naval Academy rejected his application. Of course, they sealed his files, but I was able to talk to the recruiter privately. He told me Noland scared the daylights out of him as well. The recruiter quit his job soon after he started receiving menacing phone calls."

"He believed Noland was behind the calls?" Hannah asked.

"Yes, in his mind, there's no doubt. They rattled him so much that he later left the state. In fact, I tried to contact him again, but he'd changed his number. I have no idea where he is now."

Cooper was beginning to see what the doctor meant. Luis Noland was one deranged individual. "Why do you think Noland killed his wife?" he asked because it didn't add up in his book. "Clearly he adored her."

The doctor took a moment to consider his answer. "He didn't express any reason for doing it. As I've said, he didn't admit to the crime, and I often wondered if this wasn't some ploy created by his legal team to get him off. After his release, I feared the worst. That he would come after me."

The doctor's glance ping-ponged between them. "His mental condition had been deteriorating for a while, apparently. Brenda had sent a note to her family. They received it after her death. She accused him of abusing her for years. Her medical records backed those claims. In the note, she seemed to indicate she'd finally mustered the courage to do something about it. The family believed she was going to leave him. She'd hinted at someone new in her life, a friend, perhaps someone from the neighborhood, since Brenda didn't work. I believe Brenda realized she didn't want to live in fear any longer. My guess is that sent Noland into a rage and he ultimately killed her."

As interesting as all of this was, they still didn't have a clue where to find Noland. "Doctor, we must find him before he kills again. Can you tell us anything about where he might be hiding? Did he mention any place in particular that he liked to go?"

The doctor scratched his chin as he considered the question. "As I've said, he refused to talk about his wife's murder or anything related to the crime. Most of our discussions were about abstract things like world conditions or sports. I do remember he was passionate about movies. Not what you'd expect, he preferred Westerns. He adored the Duke. He'd seen every one of his movies. I told him once he could watch John Wayne anytime online, but he insisted he preferred seeing the Duke's movies on the big screen only." The doctor shook his head. "He could recite them by heart. John Wayne's work was one of the few movies the institute allowed the patients to see. Luis was in heaven then. It's not much, I realize."

The doctor sensed Cooper's growing frustration. "I'm sorry. Really, I wish I had more, but Noland was an enigma. He kept his secrets close."

Cooper had never felt so discouraged. He got to his feet. "Thank you for seeing us, doctor."

Hoffman stood as well. "There is one more thing. Last year before I was fired, Noland checked himself back into the hospital for a short stay. He wanted more treatment. Needless to say, the new doctor was thrilled. He thought it proved everything I said was wrong. In my mind, it was suspicious at best. Noland hated his time at Brookhaven. He wouldn't have come back without reason. I have a feeling he wanted back there to check out medical records again."

The doctor's glasses slipped from his forehead. He smiled briefly and positioned them back on his nose. "Ah, I wondered where these had gone."

Cooper turned to Hannah. "Can you give us a minute? It's a private matter."

Though clearly curious, Hannah didn't question Cooper. "I'll wait outside." She thanked Hoffman for his time.

Cooper waited for the door to close before asking, "What can you tell me about cellular memories? Are they real or just some claims by desperate people?" He had to figure out if what Hannah was experiencing in her dreams was real or just part of the stress she'd been under lately.

"Why do you ask?" the doctor lifted his brows, clearly curious. "Is this connected to the case in some way?"

Cooper decided he trusted the man. He told the doctor about Hannah's dreams. That she recognized her donor as well as Noland from them.

"Ah, well, I've done extensive research in the field because it is fascinating to me." The doctor sounded intrigued. "I've interviewed many recipients who claimed to have their donor's memories. In my opinion, their claims were real, at least to them. Hang on a second. I have some information that I published in the *Psychiatry Today Journal* a few years back. It might help you understand what your friend is dealing with." The doctor dug through a stack of papers until he found the magazine in question.

"Here we go." He handed Cooper the magazine. "It amazed me to learn how many cases there are where heart transplant recipients possess memories attributed to their donor. I found an entire website dedicated to cellular memories. It's listed on page five. There you can read about case after case of recipients recounting specific memories from their donors' lives."

"Thanks for this." Cooper held up the magazine while feeling overwhelmed. "I'll pass it on to my friend. I think she'll be relieved to hear she's not alone." Although he knew Hannah had this information already. Once they said their goodbyes, Cooper stepped outside where Hannah waited next to the SUV.

"What was that about?" Hannah asked once they were on their way.

Cooper told her what the doctor said.

Her huge eyes showed shock. "You had no right to discuss my medical information with someone else."

He clasped her hand. "I know and I'm sorry, but I just wanted a professional opinion on the matter. For now, let's focus on finding Noland."

She blew out an angry breath. "You're right. He's dangerous." She paused for a long moment. "Unfortunately, the good doctor didn't give us much else to go on, did he?"

Cooper had to agree. "No, but as soon as we get back to the hotel, I want to check around the local movie theaters that show old movies. Let's see if John Wayne is playing anywhere."

CHAPTER THIRTY

"S Cooper entered the conference room and saw the solemn omething's wrong." Hannah sensed it the moment she and expressions on their team's faces.

"What's going on?" Hannah asked as she and Cooper went over to the group gathered in the middle of the room.

"Detective Siegler is missing." Jack told them how Chief Milam reached out. "Kate wasn't responding to her radio. He arrived at her house. There are signs of a struggle. Some of her clothing is missing."

"He's taken her." Hannah turned to Cooper. Embalmer had taken a police officer right from her home.

"Sierra, Zeke, and I are heading over to her house now." Jack reached for his jacket. "Detective Jordan's there already."

"She won't have long. We need to figure out where he's taking his victims." Cooper swiped a hand across his neck. "Hannah and I will keep looking into that."

Jack nodded before following his team out.

"This has to be connected to your great-grandparents' house somehow." Hannah took off her jacket while trying to push aside the frightening things they'd learned about Luis Noland.

"I agree, but we searched the property. The house. There's nothing."

"We missed something. He takes them there somewhere." Hannah grabbed Zeke's laptop. "Zeke has the survey of the property."

Cooper sat down beside her. "Any news on Pete Albertson's whereabouts or the rest of the family?"

Megan looked up from her computer. "Nothing yet. I'm working on it now. Did you find out anything helpful from the doctor?"

Cooper told her what they'd learned about Noland and about Hannah's dreams.

Megan abandoned what she'd been working on. "You really think those dreams could be cellular memories manifesting themselves?"

Hannah wasn't sure what she hoped for. That her heart's memories had been trying to tell her something through the years or that she'd imagined the whole thing.

She'd enlarged the satellite photo of Cooper's family's property and had begun searching every square inch of the landscape while Cooper leaned over her shoulder.

"Wait—what's that?" He pointed to a spot past the apple orchard.

"I see it, and I have no idea." Hannah blew the photo up more until they could make it out. "It looks like some type of ventilation pipe going into the ground . . . Cooper, he's keeping them underground." "Let's go." Cooper rose quickly.

"Go, I'll call the police and let Jack know," Megan said.

Hannah shoved her arms into her coat and carried the laptop with the exact location of the pipe on the map as they raced from the hotel.

Cooper pulled away from the portico. "I have a bad feeling about this." He spared her a look. "I hope we reach her in time."

Hannah felt the same way. "There's a different entrance to the property than from where we went in before."

She pointed it out on the screen. Cooper nodded. "I remember playing back there as a kid."

Her cell phone rang. "It's Doctor Hoffman." Hannah answered the call on speaker. "Did you remember anything further?" Blood-curdling screams filled the air.

"Doctor Hoffman?"

As the screams continued, the call suddenly went dead. Hannah tried the number several times without answer. "I'm calling the local police." She dialed the number. As soon as the dispatcher answered, she identified herself and gave the doctor's address. "We believe he's under attack." The dispatcher assured her officers were on their way.

"Please have them call me as soon as they know anything." Hannah ended the call. Her first instinct was to rush to the doctor's house, but they had another serial killer to catch.

Cooper reached for her hand. "You did everything you could. It's up to the police now."

"I just hope he's alright." The terror in his voice told her the doctor was far from okay.

They passed the turnoff to Cooper's great-grandparents' house and circled around until they reached the back side of the property.

"There." Hannah pointed to the opening. A single set of tire tracks confirmed someone had been there recently.

"We should wait for backup," Hannah warned.

"He could get away. We can't risk it." Cooper turned onto the drive and sped down it. "How close are we to the pipe?"

"Head to the left." Hannah guessed about a quarter mile away.

"I see it." Cooper slowed down and stopped near the pipe.

Hannah called Zeke. "Where are you guys?"

"Ten minutes out. Don't go in, Hannah. Wait for us."

"Hurry." She ended the call. Both got out and went over to the pipe.

Cooper knelt. "It sounds like there's a generator running."

"He has power down there." Her heart rate went ballistic. "There's no vehicle."

Cooper looked around. "You're right. Maybe he's not here after all."

"I don't see an entrance." She shielded her eyes against the sun and searched the countryside. "There's a group of trees over there." They both headed toward them.

Down the drive sirens blared. She noticed the black SUV leading the way followed by a multitude of police officers. Thank goodness. Their backup had arrived.

Jack and the rest of the team, along with the police officers, spotted them and came over.

"What are you thinking?" Jack asked.

"There has to be a hidden entrance somewhere." Cooper told him about the generator.

"I've got something over here." Sierra waved them over to where she and one of the officers stood.

"What is it?" Hannah asked as they reached them.

A downed tree had been rolled away from its resting place to reveal what appeared to be some type of camouflage covering.

Cooper lifted the cover. "There's a door."

It appeared to be made of steel.

"It's locked." Sierra pointed to the heavy-duty padlock.

"Stand back." Chief Milam waited until everyone was away from the area before he fired. The bullets didn't harm the lock. "I need bolt cutters."

One of his officers returned to a patrol car and retrieved a set of bolt cutters.

The officer cut the lock. Whatever was down there, someone didn't want it found.

Once the destroyed lock was removed, Chief Milam opened the door.

"There's a camera." Zeke pointed above the door to the small light flashing. "We're being watched."

"He's not here." Hannah told them.

"Be careful, everyone." Jack warned the team. "We don't know what we'll find down there."

A sense of apprehension settled into the pit of Hannah's stomach as Chief Milam stepped inside. "There's a light switch." He clicked it on. Startling bright light filled the space. A set of stairs led underground.

Once they reached the floor below, Hannah realized there was something familiar about the space. It was set up like a living room from years ago.

"I know this place." She looked around at the pieces of furniture and realized how. "This was in one of the photos from Oliver's childhood."

Cooper's eyes widened as he saw what she did. "You're right. The one photo from inside that house in Pennsylvania."

Hannah noticed a photo on an end table. "Look at this." She picked it up and showed it to Cooper. "That's your father and his siblings."

"He recreated the inside of the house. Maybe it represented happier times for him."

"Let's search every inch." Jack gave the order.

"What is this place?" Hannah whispered.

"I don't know. It's creepy, right?" Cooper reached for her hand as they started down a hallway. There was only one door at the end. The humming of the generator grew louder.

"There are cameras everywhere." Cooper pointed to the walls where they were mounted near the ceiling. "He wanted to keep tabs on the place." Another lock proved as difficult as the first.

Chief Milam hesitated. "I don't like this. Everybody back up." He waited until they fell back before breaking open the lock with bolt cutters.

Hannah half-expected the place to explode. She blew out a relieved breath when nothing happened.

The team spread out in the long room that had been decorated in the same fashion as the rest of the place.

"It's a bedroom," Cooper said in disbelief. He still held her hand.

There were several beds around the space.

"Oh no . . ." Hannah wasn't even aware of saying the words. Her shock became an almost physical repulsion when she realized there were bodies lying in all the beds.

Zeke lowered his weapon and closed the space to the first bed. "They've been here for a while. They're . . . mummified."

Hannah slowly followed him over to the first bed, where a woman was dressed in footed pajamas. "This must be Oliver's sisters." Four girls. All at different ages of maturity. One appeared to be in her late forties. From Hannah's assessment, she'd died recently.

"Y-you've got to see this." Jack's shocked tone reached out. He stood on the opposite side of the room, where a man stood.

Cooper's labored footsteps carried him to the impossible.

"Is that . . . ?" Hannah whispered in a strangled tone.

Cooper dropped to his knees and stared into the sightless eyes of a real-life monster. "That's my father."

Oliver Ellison had been found. Resting alongside his sisters.

CHAPTER THIRTY-ONE

They'd found his family. He watched federal agents walking around his special place and realized he wasn't angry. In fact, it was almost freeing. Mentor was gone from his head. He was completely in control.

He clicked off the video screen. They were his past. The future waited. *She* waited for him. Now, there would be no more Mentor pointing out everything he did wrong.

Finding them hadn't been as easy as Tonya. She'd been close to him since they'd ended up at the same orphanage, even though they lost touch for a while.

Before he'd reconnected with Mentor, he'd carefully tracked each one down. Most had been happy to see him. They were just as twisted as their old man. Oliver might have made a name for himself as the Embalmer, but he certainly wasn't the first. Their father had perfected the art of torture on his children. Until he'd taken him out.

The space that he'd created for them to rest was exactly like their old homeplace but different because it lacked the devil who had lived there.

No! He wouldn't let Mentor back into his head. He'd taken care of his father. His mother lived because she was just as broken as the others.

He'd felt sorry for Tonya. They had a connection. She'd needed him to survive when they'd both ended up at the same orphanage. He'd done his best to protect her from their past through the years, but she was just too damaged, and she'd gone to the FBI to turn him in. And so, he'd killed her and gave her a final resting place with the others in his family. Now that he was truly free of his ugly past, he'd set about finding more suitable family members.

Stopping in front of the two-way mirror, he noticed her waking. So pretty. She would make a wonderful addition to the family. He'd feel protected with her close. Now that he had her, there would be only one sister missing to replace his real sisters. Next, he'd search for brothers.

Inside the secured room, her eyes popped open. She yanked against her restraints. He hurried to unlock the door before she injured herself.

When he entered the room, she stopped and tried to understand where she knew him from.

He smiled to reassure her.

"How are you feeling?"

Her eyes widened as if she couldn't believe he'd ask her the question.

"I know you."

She recognized him. That made him happy. "That's right. We've met several times." He came over to where she sat in her chair.

"You were at the restaurant the other day."

He chuckled in delight at her memory. He'd left an impression. So had she.

"We have a lot to talk about. I hope you'll be comfortable here."

Once more she tried to free herself. "Do you have any idea how much trouble you're in?"

He knitted his brow, her anger confusing. "No, there's no trouble."

She leaned forward. "I'm a police officer. There are dozens of law enforcement officers looking for me right now."

He shook his head. "They won't find you. Now, let's not talk about such things when we should be getting to know each other."

She wouldn't give up so easily. He looked forward to the challenge she'd present.

He pulled up a chair. "Are you hungry? I made us dinner."

She stared at him as if he were some strange bug who repulsed her. "Let me go while you still can."

He made a tsking sound with his tongue. "That's not going to happen. We're going to get to know each other better, and then I'm going to make you part of my family forever."

Her eyes flashed shock. "I will never be part of your family, you sick —"

Fury rose inside him at the insult that matched his father's ridicule. He grabbed the syringe from his pocket and jabbed it into her neck. Surprise turned to fear as she stared at him in horror.

He'd been wrong. She wasn't worthy of immortality. She was just as bad as his sister. The unworthy had no place here in his perfect family home.

CHAPTER THIRTY-TWO

"Hteam just outside the underground bunker while ERT and e's dead." Hannah returned to Cooper, who stood near the the medical examiner worked inside. "Doctor Hoffman was stabbed to death."

Cooper shifted toward her. "Noland must have been watching when we went to Hoffman's place."

Hannah struggled to shake off the murder. "The police will get in touch if they find anything useful. They're still searching for Noland. And there's no record of a movie theater showing any John Wayne movies."

She watched as the first of the victims was brought out. "How are you handling all this?" Her hand swept the entrance.

"Believe it or not, I'm relieved. Knowing my father survived and was out there living his life after what he did to my mother, well, it was unthinkable."

She could certainly understand. "So, Pete tracked his siblings down and killed them one by one. Brought them here to keep them and visit from time to time? That's sick."

Cooper's mouth thinned. "They were damaged. From what I've read about Larry Albertson, he was a sociopath who did a number on everyone he came in contact with, including his kids and his wife."

Many of the siblings suffered from drug addictions—including Tonya the youngest and last to die. Several had mental issues throughout their lives. They'd found Tonya's burner phone on her person. She was the one Cooper had spoken to. She'd tried to do the right thing, and, in the end, it had gotten her killed.

"What happened to the mother, I wonder?" Hannah asked.

"She died of natural causes after marrying her fourth husband."

"What a sad story. So many lives were destroyed because of one man's abuse."

One by one the bodies were removed until the last—Oliver Ellison—was placed into the back of the ambulance that would take him to the medical examiner's office.

Once Oliver was loaded, the medical examiner spoke with the team.

"Any idea how long he's been dead?" Cooper motioned toward the ambulance.

Doctor Ilene Younger gave him a best guess of years. "But one of the female victims died more recently."

"That was Tonya. How recent?" Hannah asked.

"Within a day or so," Doctor Younger told her. "I'll know more once I get them on my table."

Jack thanked her. "Keep us apprised."

"That was a drain on time we don't have, and Detective Siegler is still missing." Chief Milam watched the ambulance leave, the frustration in his voice clear.

"You're right." Jack ran his hand across his eyes. "We can safely rule this property out as the Embalmer's trophy location. Where else would he keep his victims? I need suggestions."

They were all frustrated. Every time it appeared they were close to discovering the truth, it faded around them.

Hannah's thoughts kept returning to the photos Fern's sister gave them. "What about the house in Pennsylvania?"

"If the house is still standing, it's less than a hundred miles away." Cooper asked Zeke if he'd located the place yet.

"I did. I'll send it to you. We should also check the house where the family moved here in New York. I have that address as well."

"Thanks. We'll need to split up to search them both in time. Cooper, you, Hannah, and Zeke go with Detective Jordan to Pennsylvania. Sierra, you're with me and the chief. We'll need as many men as you can spare." Jack waited for Chief Milam's confirmation before addressing his people again. "Be careful. No one does anything without their team." His gaze landed on Hannah. "That goes double for you."

Zeke took over the helm of the Armada while Detective Jordan rode shotgun.

Hannah settled in the back seat along with Cooper. She was tired and pushing herself harder than she should.

"You okay?" Cooper asked, noticing her exhaustion.

"I'm fine. Just the case. Noland." She had a bad feeling that she and Noland would meet again. And soon.

CHAPTER THIRTY-THREE

He stormed from the house because he needed fresh air to clear his head. She'd made him angry. He'd imagined their conversation going quite differently. They'd share stories of their lives. He'd laugh when she told a joke. They'd bond, and he'd welcome her into his family. Instead, she'd insulted him. Looked at him as if he were crazy.

He'd taken several steps before he stopped and drew in a handful of breaths. Turning toward the house, he sniffed the air like an animal. Had he made a mistake? Mentor had always been there to guide him to the right victim. What if he couldn't do it alone?

"You don't need him," he growled and raked his hand through his hair. He'd give her another chance. Perhaps they'd just gotten off to a bad start. That happened sometimes when two strong personalities adjusted to each other.

A slow smile spread across his face. "Yes, that has to be it." He didn't need Mentor. He'd never needed Mentor.

He'd been furious with her. In his eyes, the list of her transgressions was endless.

Last night's sin was forgetting to bake the bread the way his mother prepared it. No, that wasn't the truth. Snuggled in her quiet corner, she'd let her mind drift to happier days while her body healed. Soon, she'd lost track of time and rushed to prepare the evening meal, but there wasn't enough time for the bread.

She could still see the monster as it emerged within him. More and more lately, the monster was in control. Soon, the man that she married would disappear forever, leaving only that evil presence in his place.

And then what?

Each time, after he beat her, he'd beg for her forgiveness, and she'd give it to him.

And the cycle continued on and on.

She carefully slipped from the bed and looked at him. He'd fallen asleep, clutching her tight against his chest as if fearing she might escape.

Did she dare follow through with her plan? She prayed for guidance. What she considered went against everything her parents taught her. Would they forgive her? Would God?

The only answer was his steady breathing and the reassurance that time was slipping away . . . and her mind was made up.

There was no stopping now. No turning back. The deed was done. The note sent. Soon, the world would know their dirty secrets. A light had illuminated the darkness. The monster that lived within its recesses couldn't survive the warmth of the light. Once it was over, the world would see the terror she'd survived. They'd understand. They had to.

But would her family? Would God? She'd prayed. Her knees were as bloody as her body was bruised. She'd done everything possible to gain God's forgiveness. It was now up to Him.

She'd been strong. She'd outsmarted him. He'd thought her simple, but she'd gotten the better of him.

The knife shook in her hand as she raised it to her neck. She'd waited until he slept to play out the final scene. For a moment, as she considered the consequences, her courage stumbled, but only for the length of time it took to say a tiny prayer and slice the knife across her throat in one swift movement.

A final smile touched her lips. She'd won. God had answered her prayers after all. The monster had met his match.

◆◆◆

A scream erupting from the woman at his side sent shivers down his spine and tore Cooper from troubled thoughts.

He reached for her. Her terrified eyes shifted his way as she fought him.

"Hannah, it's okay. It's me—Cooper."

Zeke jerked the SUV over onto the shoulder. He turned in his seat with the same fear in his eyes. "Hannah, what is it? What's wrong?"

Hannah struggled to speak while her eyes shimmered with tears. Her breathing frantic.

"I'm okay," Hannah finally managed to get words out. "I'm okay."

Cooper stared into the face of terror and didn't believe her. He couldn't get what she and Doctor Hoffman had told him out of his head. The documentation he'd read recounted various case studies indicating that heart recipients sometimes retained certain memories from their donors. Was it possible Brenda Noland, Luis's murdered wife, was reaching out to Hannah in the only way possible to convict her husband? The very thought settled uncomfortably around him.

Hannah covered her face with her hands, struggling for calm. "It was awful. It didn't feel like a dream. Her terror and her desperation were palpable. It was almost as if she were trying to tell me something important."

"It's going to be alright," Zeke said, clearly concerned for his sister. "I'm not going to let that guy close to you."

She slowly smiled and leaned forward to squeeze his shoulder. "You've always had my back." She looked around at the gathering shadows of late afternoon. "Where are we?"

"Almost to the house in Sugar Grove. Just a few more miles."

Hannah glanced behind them at the police cruiser traveling with them. The driver had pulled over, waiting for them.

Detective Jordan got out to update his people.

"Any news from Jack?" The house near Rochester would be closer. They should know something by now.

Cooper shook his head. "Nothing so far, but they're still searching."

"I sure hope we find her in time."

He squeezed her arm. "Me too."

Detective Jordan returned, and they continued on their way. Cooper watched the woods on either side of the road with a sense of unease. "Looks like our backup is here." The local PD met them near the house. Zeke brought the SUV to a halt behind one of the two police vehicles.

Everyone got out and went over.

"Any sign of movement?" Cooper asked the police officer in charge.

"Nothing as far as we've noticed. We've been here for a while."

The gathering darkness would help them keep their approach secret unless the killer had cameras set up around the property like he had at Cooper's old homeplace.

"Let's go." Cooper resisted the urge to warn Hannah to stay close. He didn't want to lose her to his father's brother—the new Embalmer. Or to Luis Noland, the man who killed his wife, Brenda. The woman whose heart Hannah possessed.

Approaching through the woods would provide the most coverage.

According to Zeke's map, the house lay another quarter mile into the woods. The property owner, Stanford Ewing, had very little known about him. His online record claimed he was a banker out of Pittsburgh. He'd bought the property a few years back.

Cooper stopped to gather his bearings. "It's certainly isolated enough."

They covered the rest of the space to the house that appeared to be in the same shape as in the photos from years earlier—dilapidated and neglected.

Zeke told them the property had been vacant for decades.

As they neared the house not a single light appeared inside. Trees and overgrown weeds had taken over the yard.

Tension tightened Cooper's shoulder blades. He didn't like it.

"Doesn't look like anyone's been here in a while," Jordan said.

"No, it doesn't, but we can't afford to overlook anything at this point. Siegler's life is on the line," Cooper said.

"We split up. Alex and I will take the back." Zeke assigned officers to go with each team.

"Ready?" he asked Hannah once Zeke's team got into position.

Maybe it was the remnants of the dream still, but he'd never seen Hannah appear so uncertain before.

She did her best to assure him.

Cooper led the way to the front of the dilapidated porch with rotted spots everywhere. He searched around for any sign of cameras. Nothing. Were they wrong?

He placed his hand on the door when he noticed it and froze. A trip wire was almost undetectable near the spot where he'd been about to place his foot. He pointed to it.

Everyone fell back. Cooper alerted Zeke.

"Same, here. I've got some knowledge of explosives. Let me take a look." Cooper stayed on the line with him. After a long, tense moment, Zeke told him he believed it wasn't wired to explosives. "Looks like a trip wire to an alarm."

"Which means he could be in there. He may know we're here. Let's breach now."

"Copy you."

Cooper opened the door carefully so as not to hit the wire. Darkness and a musky scent seemed to indicate the place hadn't been lived in in years.

Zeke confirmed his team entered from the rear.

Cooper didn't want to use any lights, but seeing more than a few inches in front of them was impossible. He clicked on his flashlight. The house looked worse in the light. Peeling wallpaper. Furniture covered in years of dust. Spots on the floor had rotted where the roof leaked.

Zeke had indicated there was a basement entrance though the kitchen. Cooper searched around for cameras. None. He didn't understand.

Cooper led the way through to the kitchen. Scurrying sounds had him imagining all sorts of rodents.

A single door led to the basement. Cooper spotted the same type of trip wire and pointed it out.

The second he opened the door, the atmosphere changed drastically. The space appeared well lit. The familiar hum of a generator confirmed a source of power.

Cooper's weapon was at the ready. Behind him, Hannah and the rest of the team followed his lead. He did his best to descend the stairs quietly. When they reached the bottom, the space was eerily familiar to the one where Ellison's family had been preserved.

A living room had been decorated similarly—the only difference was it contained a kitchen.

A coffeepot held coffee. He touched the pot. Still warm. Someone had been here recently.

Cooper indicated the coffee as a warning.

As they advanced down the hall, doors on either side showed another difference. One stood open. A bedroom. The Embalmer lived here.

At the final door another trip wire. Cooper pulled in a breath before opening the door.

The door barely opened when someone charged toward them wielding a knife. Cooper didn't have time to dodge before the man slashed his shoulder. The force of the attack dropped Cooper to his knees.

Someone fired. Cooper's attacker fell beside him.

Hannah rushed over and knelt beside Cooper and examined the wound. "It's not so bad." A trickle of blood spread across his shirt sleeve.

Cooper struggled to his feet. He and Hannah went over to where the man lay. He'd been shot through the upper torso.

Zeke examined the wound. "He's in bad shape." One of the local police called for medical assistance.

While Zeke did his best to keep the man alive, Cooper looked around at their surroundings and couldn't believe what he was seeing. Several "rooms" had been set up. Inside each was a different woman. He recognized Tiffany and Veronica. Above the embalmed women were other names. The names of Pete's sisters.

"She's not displayed. Siegler's here somewhere." He ran down the hallway and noticed there were two vacant spots. One for Siegler and one for the final sister.

Cooper reached a door and opened it. Jordan and Hannah along with a bunch of officers went with him.

Another hallway. A window was on the left side. It reflected a room. Kate Siegler was slumped over in a chair where she'd been restrained.

"Kate!" Jordan quickly opened the door and rushed to Siegler's side. He felt for a pulse. "She's still alive." Jordan removed her restraints. "Kate. Wake up."

"Needle marks on her neck. He's drugged her. Where's our ambo?" Hannah called out.

"Two minutes out." One of the officers confirmed. Soon, several EMTs entered the room. Pete was stabilized for transport to the hospital. Siegler regained consciousness and tried to refuse medical treatment, but her partner insisted she was going to the hospital, and Jordan went with her.

Cooper and the rest of the team stepped out to let ERT work.

"You should let the EMTs take a look at your shoulder," Hannah urged as she followed him outside.

"It's superficial. There's a first-aid kit in the car."

As they headed through the woods, Cooper couldn't believe what they'd discovered. Pete Albertson was a sick person. His troubled childhood had led him to want to replace his family with a new one of his choosing.

He had a feeling the more they dug into this brother, the more terrifying his personality would become.

Someone stepped from the shadows. Cooper thought it was one of their people until Hannah was struck by the branch the man wielded. Her weapon went flying from her hand. Before he could get his weapon out of the holster, the man lunged for him with a knife, plunging it into his chest. The force sent him flying backwards. He barely registered Hannah screaming his name. As he fell forward more blows came. His last thought was for Hannah. He'd promised to protect her. He'd failed.

CHAPTER THIRTY-FOUR

Luis Noland stood over Cooper with the knife poised to kill. Hannah's reactions were slower than they should have been.

"Please don't," she screamed. All she could think about was Cooper. Was he still alive? She loved him. And Cooper was bleeding out.

"Brenda?"

Hannah felt sick. The very sight of the man who had caused so much pain revolted her. Brenda had suffered much at his hand, but she had to be strong. Only the tiniest of movements from Cooper was enough to tell her he was still alive, if only barely.

Where was her weapon? Cooper's was still in its holster. She needed to think rationally. Needed to reach out to Luis in the only way possible— as Brenda.

Cooper's life depended on it.

"Yes, it's me. You've found me at last."

His face crumpled with emotion. "I didn't mean to hurt you. Why did you write that note? Why did you tell them I killed you, Brenda? It wasn't me; it was you."

Hannah barely recognized the voice as human. Shocked, it finally made sense. Noland hadn't taken his wife's life. Brenda's death had come at her own hands and had been by her own choosing.

"I know the truth. I'm here now. It wasn't your fault."

He stepped closer—away from Cooper, the knife he clutched in his hand nicking at his leg.

Could she reach Cooper's weapon in time?

Luis seemed unaware of the blood seeping through his pants. "I never told anyone. Not a soul. I did it for you, Brenda. I called an ambulance. They came, took you to the hospital. They said they couldn't save you, but they were able to salvage your organs. They stole your heart. I hunted for it. Nothing would stop me from finding it and you. I knew we'd be together again."

"Yes." She stepped closer to Cooper while trying to keep Noland's attention on her. Cooper barely managed to get his weapon from the holster, but he was fading fast. He had lost a tremendous amount of blood.

Hannah had her phone in her hand and called Zeke. She put the phone on speaker for her brother to hear.

She heard Zeke ask her what was wrong.

Noland heard. "What are you doing? You called someone?" He noticed the phone. When he focused on her, it appeared as if he realized she wasn't his wife. "You're not my Brenda. My Brenda wouldn't betray me like that." He raised the knife and lunged for Hannah.

She sidestepped the attack and grabbed Cooper's weapon. Hannah fired off two shots. The first grazed the left side of his ear. The second hit its mark dead on. Straight through the heart of a killer.

Noland crashed to the ground like a rock, mere inches from Hannah. She kicked the knife from his reach, checked for a pulse, and didn't find one.

Then she rushed to Cooper's side. Hannah removed her coat and tried to stop the bleeding.

"Zeke, get EMTs down here now. Cooper's been attacked," she yelled into the phone and gave their location.

Cooper's eyes were open, but he couldn't speak because one of the blows had slashed his throat. She squeezed his hand as her eyes filled with tears. "Hang in there. Help is on the way. They'll be here soon. Don't give up. Don't you dare give up."

The faint squeeze against her hand was her only answer.

CHAPTER THIRTY-FIVE

Two weeks later—BAU Headquarters, Quantico, Virginia—0900 hours

As soon as he stepped into the room, applause erupted. Cooper smiled, though a bit embarrassed. He didn't much like having attention solely on him. There'd been enough of that lately.

He searched the room for her. She wasn't there.

Zeke enveloped him in a hug that had Cooper wincing. "Glad to have you back, Coop."

"Good to be back. Where's Hannah?" he said loud enough for only Zeke to hear.

"She's taking some time." Zeke didn't look him in the eye.

Questions flew through his head. He couldn't ask any of them now.

"Coop!" Jane gave him a hug then looked him over. "You don't appear any worse for the wear considering you died." "Almost died," Cooper corrected her.

After each had greeted him, Cooper slipped into one of the chairs, the excursion exhausting. Since the stabbing, his energy level was next to none.

"A lot has happened since you've been gone," Jack told him. "And we have more details about Pete Albertson."

"Okay." Cooper dreaded the news to come. There had been a tidal wave of bad news since the Embalmer case resurrected itself.

Jack opened a folder and looked Cooper in the eye. "Are you sure you're ready to hear this?"

Cooper forced himself to confirm he was.

"For reasons we don't know, Pete adored your old man. They connected off and on through the years. The most recent was a few months before Ellison was arrested."

"So, my father knew exactly where Pete was and that he'd be there for him after he faked his death."

"Exactly. I think they had a rough plan for his escape before he was even arrested. We can't prove it, but it's possible Pete may have assisted his brother with the previous murders."

"Unbelievable. Did they find out what happened to the father who started all this insanity?" Cooper wouldn't let his father or Pete excuse their behavior because they'd suffered unimaginable things. Others had gone through the same nightmare and hadn't turned into serial killers.

"He pretty much dropped off the face of the earth about fifteen years after the siblings' mother was arrested for drug possession."

"Pete killed him," Cooper deducted from Jack's expression.

"Probably, but we don't have any proof of that. The mother, Elizabeth, went through several marriages. She never tried to get her children back from the state. I think she was just as messed up as the siblings by Bruce Albertson's reign of terror."

A part of Cooper actually felt sorry for the kid his father had been back then. For Pete and the others.

Megan took up the story. "We found out why there was no DNA match to you for Pete. He wasn't actually Oliver's brother but a cousin who was taken in by Elizabeth. Oh, and get this—Elizabeth had dark hair and a similar build as the victims. I guess even though she was a drug addict and an unfit mother, Pete and Oliver still loved her."

While Cooper tried to digest this piece of information, Megan continued. "Anyway, since Oliver knew the Ellisons and they felt sorry for him, they took him in and later adopted him. By then, the other children had been placed in foster homes or orphanages."

Cooper had to know the truth. "Did Oliver or perhaps Pete kill the Ellisons?"

Megan shook her head. "We don't have any proof, but I'd say it's likely. Oliver had the most to gain."

Zeke shoved away from the wall where he stood and sat beside Cooper. "Tonya was the baby of the family. It appears Pete tried to protect her most of her life, and yet she fell into drug use. He found out she called us and killed her soon after. We located her trailer house. Pete wrote unworthy on the wall and then snitch." Zeke shook his head.

Cooper was in shock. "What about Pete? Did he survive?"

Jack nodded. "He's alive. He's not talking. We've tried to interview him with his attorney, but he's not making any sense. I'd say it's an act to get found unfit to stand trial, but, in this instance, I actually believe he is mentally unfit. He keeps talking about Mentor as if he's a real person. We believe Mentor is Oliver, his brother."

"Oh, and there's good news on Isobel." Sierra covered his hand with hers. "She's awake and talking. She's helped us fill in a lot of the pieces." She hesitated.

"Just say it." Whatever she didn't want to tell him couldn't be any worse than what he knew about his family so far.

Sierra glanced to Megan who nodded. "Isobel said when Pete took her to your family's basement he had your father with him."

He'd been wrong. This was far worse. "How is that possible? How long has my father been dead?"

"More than ten years, according to the medical examiner." Jack flipped to the report. "He was injected with the same type of concoction given to the worthy victims. Cooper, Pete took your father with him on his hunts for victims. Isobel said he talked to him as if he were still alive. As I've said, he's delusional."

"What about Luis Noland? Did he know Pete? Were the two cases connected at all?" Cooper wasn't sure which one he hoped for. That the deranged man targeting Hannah might be working with Pete, or that they were two separate cases, which confirmed more than ever the existence of true evil.

"They aren't connected," Jack told him. "There's no record the two ever crossed paths. But we did look into other transplant recipients of Brenda's organs. Several were brutally murdered." Jack hesitated. "He cut them open. He was looking for Brenda's heart."

Cooper's stomach turned. "That's one sick individual." There were more questions he should be asking, and yet all Cooper could think about was Hannah. She'd left him without so much as a goodbye, and he had to find her.

He staggered to his feet. All eyes were on him. "I-I'm a little tired, I guess. I think I'll head out." He grabbed the door and yanked it open.

"Coop, wait up."

Cooper slowly turned and waited for Zeke to catch up with him.

"She just left without a word." The bitter emotions behind those words couldn't be hidden.

Zeke slowly smiled. "She did. She's mixed up inside."

Cooper's mouth twisted. "Yeah, well, I can't change her mind." He started to leave when Zeke grabbed his arm.

Cooper closed his eyes before facing his friend again.

"You're the only one who can change her mind. Go get her, Cooper. Bring her back where she belongs. Back with her family."

Cooper glanced past Zeke and noticed the entire team standing there cheering him on.

He suppressed a smile. "Where is she?"

"Montana."

Cooper wasn't surprised. Hannah used to talk about living in Montana one day. Having a ranch and maybe a yellow dog. Suddenly, an idea took life. Could he?

"Go, Cooper. We need her back here," Megan told him.

"And she needs you." Zeke held his gaze. "She loves you, buddy. She needs you, and you need her too."

EPILOGUE

Two days later—near Billings, Montana or the first time in a long time

there were no more troubled dreams. Hannah believed Brenda was

finally at rest. But Hannah was far from it. The peace she'd been

F searching for here in Montana hadn't

come. Mostly because one person wouldn't let her go. Cooper.

Outside, the noise of a vehicle traveling down the gravel road near her place caught her attention. Cars were rare in this part of Big Sky Country.

After shooting Luis Noland and working the Embalmer case, Hannah realized her body was worn out. She needed rest. Deep down physical and mental rest. The kind she could get only away from DC. She'd told Jack and Megan she was going away for a while. She'd asked them to keep her abreast of what happened with the case, and they had.

After making sure Cooper would make a full recovery, she'd traveled to Montana to a small rental house in the middle of a thousand-acre ranch. She'd come for peace along with rest. So far, she hadn't found it.

The vehicle had turned off the county road onto her drive. She had no doubt who had found her. Zeke would have told him where to come.

Outside, a car door opened. Instead of a knock on her door, her old porch swing creaked as if someone sat on it. Just like Cooper.

Hannah stepped outside. Her heart dropped to the pit of her stomach. Cooper sat swinging on the rickety porch swing, a big yellow dog at his feet.

She couldn't move for the longest time. Couldn't seem to draw in enough air.

Hannah forced down the tiniest bit of hope.

He didn't seem nearly as rattled by her presence as she was by his.

"Hannah." His smile was as handsome as she remembered. Infectious. Reminding her of the old Cooper before facing the darkness he'd gone through recently. And her breaking his heart.

Her lips twitched. Unable to fight it, she grinned. "Cooper. This is a surprise."

He rose and came to her. "Really?" He was close enough for her to smell his aftershave. She wanted to draw him into her arms and never let go, but first she wanted to hear his reasons for coming.

"Really. What brings you to Montana?"

His smile disappeared, and the look he gave her tore at her heart. "You just left. You're not answering my calls again. I thought we were beyond that."

It was hard not to lean up and kiss away his worries, throw caution away, but she had questions that required answers. "You know why."

He slowly nodded without looking away. "And I don't care."

With a ragged breath, he drew her into his arms and held her close. "I love you, Hannah, and I want to be with you. I don't care if it's a week, a month, a year." He touched her jaw, her mouth, with his lips confirming those words. "Don't turn me away, Hannah. Don't deny you love me too."

She pulled away, as affected by their kiss as Cooper. She needed to bring things back under control.

"Who's your friend?" She pointed to the golden retriever who sat watching their exchange with only a mild interest.

"Buster. He's a rescue dog. He used to work on a ranch, but he hurt his leg so his owner gave him over for adoption. I remembered you told me once that you wanted a yellow dog."

She smiled and tried not to set her happiness free. "Hello, Buster. Nice to meet you." She hesitated then said, "I'm glad you came."

"Thank you. I'm glad I came and that you're glad I'm here."

But there were things that needed to be said. "You need to be sure of what you're getting yourself into, Cooper, because I couldn't bear it if you change your mind."

"I won't change my mind about you or us." He cupped her face. He was going to kiss her again, but she still had questions. She pulled away. "I need you to listen. I had a heart transplant. Do you realize what that means?"

"I don't—not fully, but I also don't care. Hannah, I love you."

"I love you too, but I'll spend the rest of my life taking medicine. Having children is probably too risky . . . and I have no idea how long I'll live or if I'll need another heart." That was the hardest part to say.

She'd finally gotten through to him. "So far, the record is thirty years for a heart recipient. It might be longer with proper care. It might not. I've had my heart for nineteen years now."

Color seeped from his face. He hadn't considered the consequences. "That doesn't change my feelings one little bit. I don't care. I love you, and I'm trusting God with the rest of it. Trust Him with me. None of us can say how long we have on this earth. We should live each day to the fullest. Love the people God has chosen to bless our lives with and trust Him with the rest. I love you. I don't want to let you go again, and I'm not worried about the future because I believe it will be okay no matter what."

Tears filled her eyes and spilled over, but she went into his arms and held him tight.

She sensed something was troubling him and asked him what.

He tried to dismiss his misgivings. "Nothing."

"No, something's bothering you. It's about the case, isn't it?"

That she'd guessed wasn't a surprise. She knew him well.

"Not my father's case, but Brenda's. I'm sure this is probably the last thing you want to talk about now, but why did she do it?"

Hannah had gone to counselling after the shooting. Still, she struggled since Noland's death to put aside Brenda's terrifying memories of that monster. They'd become little more than fragmented pieces that made her think the small part of Brenda that still existed inside her had gone away.

"You mean why'd she kill herself?"

He nodded.

"I think she believed it was her only way out, otherwise he'd kill her. In the end, she took the matter out of his hands. She reclaimed some control over her life."

Cooper told her there had to be more, surely.

After a moment, Hannah shook her head. "No. By killing herself the way she did, Brenda was certain her death would get blamed on Noland. She'd obviously researched it thoroughly. She'd read all the statistics that say most women never take their lives by violent means. Brenda was smart. Much smarter than her husband gave her credit. She believed Noland was escalating in his violence toward her and she believed he might harm others. Brenda knew he would if he remained free. In her mind, this was the only way to prevent that from happening."

Hannah inhaled a deep breath. "I don't agree with what she did—all life is precious and God-given, but I understand how hopeless she felt. She believed if he were in prison somewhere, even though she couldn't save herself, she would save Noland's next victim. Or so she thought. I guess the outcome wasn't as she'd planned."

Cooper held her tighter. "No one predicted the verdict in finding him mentally incompetent to stand trial. Brenda did her part by planting the seed of abuse in her family's minds."

Hannah shivered as some of the vivid images of horror Brenda had endured crept into her thoughts. She closed her eyes and held Cooper closer.

He appeared to hesitate before asking, "Will you stay here or come back to DC? Wherever you are, I want to be."

"I'm ready to go home. Ready to spend the rest of my life with you, Cooper." Hannah twisted in his arms to see his face. "But only if you'll have me."

"I love you, Hannah," Cooper said and held her tight in his arms. "I want to be with you. Now, and however long God gives us together."

ABOUT THE AUTHOR

USA Today Bestselling Author Mary Alford loves to give her readers the unexpected. Combining unforgettable characters with unpredictable plots that result in stories the reader will not want to put down.

Her titles have appeared on the USA Today Bestsellers list twice, the Publisher's Weekly bestselling list multiple times as well as the Parable bestsellers list, and the 2023 Family Fiction Top 20 Christian Suspense Authors list!

Her book, Among the Innocent, was selected as the AWSA 2023 Golden Scroll Mystery/Suspense Novel of the Year!

Mary's books have also been finalists in the Daphne Du Maurier award of excellence in mystery, The Beverly, The Maggie, and The Selah Awards.

Mary is a member of the ACFW, and the Blue Ridge Reader Connections. She also participates in two blogs; Suspense Sisters, a blog that promotes Christian suspense, and Christians Read, a blog that discusses Christian books as well as the spiritual journey.

Mary is an avid reader. She loves to cook and can't face the day without coffee. She and her husband live in the heart of Texas in the middle of 70 acres with their sweet rescue dog Cody.

You can learn more about Mary on most social media outlets and on her website: www.MaryAlford.net.